Second Chances

Leigh Brown & Victoria Corliss

For our mothers, Kash and Nancy.

* * *

A man is like a novel: until the very last page you don't know how it will end. Otherwise it wouldn't be worth reading.
-Yevgeny Zamyatin, We

PROLOGUE

The young woman gazed out the airplane window at the clouds floating carelessly below and wondered what the future held for her and her unborn child. Rubbing her temples with her index fingers, she tried to command a "happily ever after" ending for them both. Easier said than done when you're on your own; only her best friend knew the real reason she'd come to the U.S. She'd managed to fool everyone else.

As the plane taxied to the gate, she rose from the cramped seat, pulling her bulky sweater tightly around her. Her stomach was small but getting bigger by the day it seemed. The elderly woman sitting next to her smiled and gestured for her to go ahead down the aisle as the baby inside her kicked vigorously.

She sighed. The baby hadn't stopped moving since the plane had taken off. She imagined it knew something important was about to happen.

"Oh, Baby'" she said quietly, "I hope you know I love you."

For a split second the baby's movements stopped as though it was listening to its mother. She rubbed her stomach gently and left the plane. Outside the airport she reached into her coat pocket, and with shaking fingers pulled out the small worry-worn card imprinted with her final destination: Horizon House of Hope for Mothers and Their Babies.

Signaling a taxi, she put her hand on her stomach one more time as she whispered, "That's what we need, Baby. We need hope." Handing her suitcase to the driver, she stepped into the cab.

* * *

The lights above her head were hot and bright making sweat bead on her forehead. A nurse fiddled with the long electrical tentacles of a monitoring machine suctioned to her stomach and chest. Hearing the continual stream of beeps signaling her baby's strong heartbeat, she relaxed slightly.

"You're progressing nicely." The nurse smiled briefly at her. "Dr. Colford thinks another hour and you should be ready to push."

"Another hour?" she thought in panic. Her contractions were coming every few minutes, each one sending an unbearable rush of pain over her abdomen. She didn't know how she was going to last another ten minutes, never mind an hour. "Oh, God," she pleaded, "Please make this baby hurry. It hurts so much."

As if the baby heard her, a new wave of pain pushed at her lower stomach and she grabbed the metal sidebars of her bed. She groaned loudly, her knuckles turning white from their grip.

"Never mind about that hour, I guess there's no time like the present," said the nurse and went in search of the doctor. He entered the room in business-like fashion. "Let's have this baby, shall we?" he said kindly.

A short time later, the fierce cries of her newborn child filled the room as the doctor handed the baby to her, "This little one refuses to be ignored." Extending her arms, she welcomed the new life into her embrace. Ten fingers, ten toes, a shock of thick hair and almond-shaped eyes like her own. The baby was perfect. Her heart broke.

"I'm sorry, dear, but it's time to say good-bye."

She looked at the nurse with tear-filled eyes, her arms trembling as she gave the child to her like a precious gift. "Wait," she called before the woman could leave the room. "I almost forgot." Reaching around her neck, she unclasped the only thing of value she had left. Her own mother had given it to her, the gold medallion of St. Barbara, the patron saint of protection.

The medallion was still warm with the heat of her body as she placed it carefully over the baby's head. "Be safe, Little One, be strong," she whispered as a fresh wave of tears overtook her. If she was doing the right thing, why did it feel so horribly wrong? "Please go," she begged the nurse, "before I change my mind."

Nodding sympathetically, the nurse left the room without another word.

CHAPTER ONE

Amelia stood at the cross-walk waiting patiently for the signal to turn from red to green and wished that life were always this easy. Imagine if every time you were about to make a wrong decision, a little red hand flew up and slapped common sense in your face, and when you chose wisely, a green light of approval waved you on. "That would be lovely," she sighed.

"What would?" asked Rose, grabbing a *Boston Crier* from a nearby newsstand. Amelia watched in amusement as her friend flipped furiously through the pages, bypassing the day's headlines for the hardcore gossip of the "Star Track" column. Rose sighed happily, drinking in her daily dose of celebrity happenings as Amelia casually sipped her first Diet Coke of the day.

"I bet you just wow clients with your vast knowledge of Beantown's movers and shakers," Amelia teased. Glancing at the tall, elegant red head beside her, she was struck as always by the confident poise and chic style that enveloped the brainiac investment analyst. Rose was smart, sophisticated, and fun. She was the consummate professional, popular with her clients; but most importantly, she was the best friend a girl could ask for. Brutally honest, she'd tell you if it was the outfit that made you look fat or if it was time to hit the gym, and fiercely loyal: "the man doesn't exist who's good enough for you." Rose was also an unabashed gossip whore.

"Maybe, maybe not," she replied casually, "but don't underestimate what you can learn from the "Star Track." For instance, did you know that the Grande Dame of authors, Pashmina Papadakis, is preparing to release a new novel that critics are already calling her next bestseller. Or that two of

Boston's most eligible bachelors were spotted 'hanging' in the dugout at last night's Red Sox game?"

"I must have missed that news alert," Amelia laughed as she tried to read over Rose's shoulder. "So who are these studs anyway?"

Handing her the paper, Rose waited patiently, unfazed by Amelia's sudden shriek or the undisguised curiosity of their sidewalk neighbors. "I'm going to call and demand a retraction. Tim's not an eligible bachelor, he's my boyfriend. Just because he's with playboy Ben doesn't mean he's one too."

"You know he's not," soothed Rose, delicately picking her words. "If anything, he's a lone wolf, nothing like you." Amelia nodded and Rose sighed. Clearly the girl was missing the point she was trying to make.

"And he hates baseball," Amelia continued, making her own case against the gossip. "And basketball, and football for that matter. Any team sport really. He's more of a one-on-one kind of guy."

"I bet," Rose snickered, stepping lightly beyond Amelia's swiping reach. "Oh, puhleeze, don't even try to act offended. The horse hair plaster we call walls is anything but sound proof, and the bedroom games you two play are anything but quiet!"

Blushing furiously, Amelia was inclined to agree. Sex was definitely not an issue for her and Tim. In fact, it was pretty damn hot. He wanted her, all the time it seemed. Not that she was complaining, she wanted him too; but sometimes she wished that they would talk a little more. Man, was that a girl thing to say or what?

Forcing her focus back to Rose, she said, "I'm sure Ben dragged him to the game. I think he's his only real friend besides me. Anyway, switching topics, I was going to tell you about Pashmina last night but I fell asleep before you got home. I guess the excitement of the day wore me out."

"So listen to this," Amelia said continuing her story. "Stuart called me into his office yesterday." Rose's full attention was on her with whiplash speed. "I know," Amelia agreed. "It scared me shitless. What could the big boss possibly have to say to me? I mean, I've been doing all right. A few small editorial projects that were solid but nothing --good or bad-- that would have brought the attention of the company president on me."

"So what did he want?"

"Well, apparently all of our senior editors are on assignment and they need someone to take on a special project. With my modest but respectable track record, Stuart thinks I can be trusted to manage Pashmina Papadakis' upcoming novel."

"Whoa, this is HUGE!" Rose cheered, giving Amelia a quick hug. "I mean, you've never worked with an author of Pashmina's stature before. Even I know she's one of the most critically acclaimed mystery writers of the century." She eyed her friend critically, "You know, word on the street is she's pretty tough, but you can probably take her."

Though shorter than the statuesque Rose by a few inches, Amelia was a natural beauty, petite and thin with a heavy curtain of white blonde hair and blue eyes that shifted hue like a mood ring with her changing emotions. She was steadfast and unflappable. Over the years, her quick thinking and fast talking had saved them both from more sticky situations than Rose wanted to think about. Yep, Amelia could handle just about anything you threw at her.

"Thanks for the vote of confidence," Amelia said dryly, "but Stuart says Pashmina's novels are so good they practically edit themselves. Translation: it's almost impossible for me to screw this up. All I have to do is support her and give her whatever she asks for. Stuart's not stupid. Why else would he entrust a superstar like Pashmina to a rookie like me?"

"Don't sell yourself short, Ms. Rookie," said Rose. "I'm sure there are plenty of unseasoned editors filling the ranks at Dewes, but Stuart chose you and probably with good reason. Maybe it's a test. Take good care of the Queen Bee and a sweet promotion could be in your future."

"Well, I'm going to need all the help I can get, starting today. I'm having lunch with Pashmina; and I don't mind telling you, I'm more than just a little nervous about it." Rose looked puzzled and Amelia tried to explain. "It's like you said, Pashmina is considered a diva among authors and it's a really big deal to be her editor. I haven't even met the woman yet and my arm pits are already sweating."

Rose pondered the situation, a small frown crinkling her usually smooth brow, and suggested, "Maybe you need to go see Minji before you meet Pashmina."

Amelia laughed. Minji was a Korean manicurist whose weekly ministration of Amelia's nails almost always included an unsolicited palm reading as well. Equally off the mark as on, Minji's prophecies, if not always accurate, at very least were entertaining and distracting. "That's not a bad idea," Amelia agreed as the light turned green and she and Rose moved forward across the street.

* * *

Glancing anxiously at her watch, Amelia power-walked the short distance from the Park Street T station to the restaurant where she was meeting Pashmina. Ten minutes early, perfect. She thought of her mother Francesca, South Carolina's own Emily Post, who had expounded upon the virtues of punctuality for most of Amelia's twenty-six years of life. Now it was ingrained in her DNA. "If you take the time to make an appointment, make it a point to show up on time," her mother would affirm daily. "It shows respect and commitment." Well here Amelia was, and with time to spare. Mom would be proud. Pulling open the glass doors, Amelia entered the restaurant.

"Hi," Amelia smiled at the hostess standing behind an elegant mahogany podium. "I have a 1:00 reservation for two under Blish."

"Yes, of course, Ms. Blish, your luncheon guest is already here. I'll show you to your table." A symphony of clinking glasses and quiet chatter muffled the sound of her heels on the gleaming hardwood floor. Amelia followed the young woman through a maze of linen-covered tables framed by rich, wood-paneled walls and sparkling crystal windows draped with red velvet and snowy white sheers. She smiled approvingly.

She had thought long and hard before choosing this location for the big meeting. First impressions spoke volumes, and she wanted an environment that would not only convey her admiration for the author but also express a bit of her own professional character. The Sommerset, a Brahmin institution frequented by the city's most influential power brokers, was just the place.

"Here we go," the hostess smiled, stepping aside for Amelia to take her seat. "Your waiter will be right with you."

"Thank you," Amelia replied.

"Thank you," echoed Pashmina. The two women looked at each other and smiled.

The hostess nodded, pleasantly surprised by the attention. From behind lowered lashes, she studied the women more closely, pondering their relationship. They were a striking pair. One was the picture of cool sophistication in a plum silk sheath that molded to her supple form like a glove to a hand, her dark hair twisted in a sleek chignon exposing the gently maturing features of her face and smooth olive skin. The other was fair and bright like a summer's day, in a tailored white linen pant suit and lavender blouse. Different, yet similar, their stylish appearance created a look of balanced harmony.

Amelia could feel Pashmina's steady gaze upon her as she adjusted her napkin in her lap and returned the look with her own unwavering stare.

Pashmina spoke first. "You're younger than I expected."

"Good genes," Amelia smiled. "But I have all the experience I need to do right by your manuscript," she hastened to assure the author. As Pashmina sipped slowly from her water goblet, it was Amelia's turn to inspect her. "You're different than I imagined as well," she said, eliciting a laugh.

"I'm sure I am if you believe all the hype. Were you expecting to have lunch with the Dragon Lady or the Medusa Mistress of Mystery, perhaps?" Pashmina laughed again at Amelia's discomfited expression, nonchalantly waving a graceful hand through the air. "Don't be embarrassed. I'm well aware of my monstrous reputation. Absurd really, but occasionally useful." She chuckled wickedly.

Intrigued, Amelia leaned forward, silently urging Pashmina to continue. "Writing is a solitary sport, the perfect profession for a self-proclaimed loner like me," she said, running a tapered finger in lazy circles around the rim of her glass. "Unfortunately, the publicity that goes along with promoting my books is always such an elaborate production," she shuddered. "I feel exposed and horribly uncomfortable. My alter egos are simply my way of coping with the evils of the necessary but unwanted attention."

A broad smile split Amelia's face. "Pay no attention to the man behind the curtain," she laughed, quoting one of her all-time favorite stories.

"Exactly!" Pashmina beamed. "Just like the Wizard of Oz, in public I'm a fearsome character, but in private, behind the curtain, I'm just Pashmina, a woman who likes to write books and be left alone."

"You're also extremely humble for a fire-breathing, snake-haired wizard," Amelia countered. "Only a handful of authors have critics and fans eating out of their hands like you do. You are truly a literary phenom." Pashmina blushed as Amelia raised her glass in silent toast.

A companionable silence settled over them as they perused the menu, selecting salads nicoise and a chilled bottle of sauvignon blanc before continuing their conversation. "I don't know if I'm hungrier for lunch or to sink my teeth into your manuscript," Amelia confessed, as a plate of colorful greens and fresh tuna was placed before her. "I've only heard enough about it to whet my appetite. Please tell me more."

"Well," Pashmina began, "I don't want to say too much or it might color your opinion of it. I'd rather you read it first and then we can discuss it ad nauseum."

"Spoken like a true woman of mystery."

"I don't mean to be. Okay, maybe a little," she laughed as Amelia rolled her eyes. "Honestly, this book is...," she paused, searching for the right word, "unlike my previous babies." She leaned towards Amelia and whispered conspiratorially, "Can I tell you a secret?"

Amelia nodded, uncertain where this was going.

"I'm so nervous, it's like I've never written before. I'm excited, but at the same time, I'm terrified too." Resting her chin on tented fingers, Pashmina studied Amelia closely. "Above all else, I need to know that my book and I are safe in your hands."

Amelia focused on piercing a minute caper with her polished fork. Fair enough. Pashmina deserved the best and she was going to get it.

Switching tactics, Amelia said, "I like how you call your books your babies."

"Mm-hmm," Pashmina replied, sipping her wine. "That's what they are to me."

"How so?"

"Well, for one thing, they've given me a lot of gray hairs over the years!" She laughed, relaxing into her chair. "They also consume my every waking moment, and sometimes my dreams too. Each one is a part of me. They're my own special creations." Emotions flitted across her face. Pride. Joy. Regret. Determination.

"I guess I never thought of it like that before. I get the love part, that's pretty obvious, but the rest sounds more like a control thing to me." Amelia chose her words carefully, feeling like she was walking in a mine field. "I mean, what parent has complete authority over their kids; the kind of people they are, the kind of lives they live? But an author just has to write it for it to happen."

"Guilty." Her mouth dry, Pashmina took a quenching sip of water from her glass. "You're very intuitive for such a young person."

"My mother always says that I'm an old soul, that the first-time she looked into my eyes she knew she'd have her hands full raising me."

Amused, Pashmina asked, "And did she?"

"I was pretty tame early on, but my teen years nearly killed us both," Amelia said dryly, and Pashmina raised a brow. "That's when I figured out that I already knew everything, and I didn't need anyone telling me what to do. But trust me," she said smiling, "my mother can give as good as she gets. As soon as she started losing control over me, she became downright militant and my worst nightmare. Suddenly I was taking swim lessons, dance lessons, piano lessons, even charm school," she shuddered remembering. "Who has time to think with that kind of schedule? That's why I came to college in Boston. I had to get away from my mother so I could figure out who I am."

As Amelia animatedly recounted her story, a captivated Pashmina listened, drawn to the vibrant young woman. With a flush of emotion lightly coloring her cheeks and a pensive gleam warming her eyes deep blue, Amelia was a vision of youthful vulnerability and quiet determination. Pashmina had no doubt, Amelia was the right woman for the job.

A while later, arms linked companionably, they exited the restaurant to a sidewalk dusted with after-work commuters scurrying to the trains and subway. "Wow. Time really does fly when you're having fun. Sorry I took so much of your time," Amelia apologized.

"Don't be silly. I had fun too, and more importantly, I think this is the beginning of a beautiful partnership."

"I'll do my best," Amelia vowed. "Thank you again for this opportunity Pashmina. I promise I won't let you down."

"I know you won't, dear," Pashmina agreed, gently patting the young woman's cheek. "Let me know when you've read the manuscript." She winked. "Then we'll really get to work!"

CHAPTER TWO

"Excuse me, Tim, it's five o'clock. Do you need anything before I leave?"

His concentration broken, Tim looked up from his desk into the vixen eyes of his secretary Jennifer who was leaning casually in the doorway of his office. Smiling suggestively, she entered the room, stopping briefly to straighten a small wall hanging. Its framed words provided the only enhancement to the otherwise impersonal space. *"Look out for number one. If you don't, no one else will."*

Tim had hung the mantra-bearing plaque himself as a constant reminder. Never lose focus. Never lose sight of your goals. No matter what or who comes along. It was that attitude that got him where he was today, a senior account executive at Trillingham Communications, the premier advertising agency in New England. And with top clients like Dewes Publishing and possibly Wilderness Stores on his roster, he was on a direct track to the 14th floor executive offices.

"So will there be anything else, or maybe we could go for a drink?" Breaking into his thoughts, Jennifer was leaning on his desk, her shapely breasts pressed together in a cleavage smile as generous as the one on her lips.

"Sorry," Tim said shaking his head regretfully. "I'm meeting Amelia for dinner."

"No worries." Smoothing her shifted top back into place, Jennifer sauntered casually out the door. "There'll be other chances."

Tim chuckled, his gaze locked appreciatively on her departing derriere as he bid a silent adieu to a no-strings night of casual fun and easy sex. No fuss, no muss that was the Tim Smith way; or was until Amelia came along.

She was something special. He had known it the minute he spotted her at a publishing party a few months back. Sparkling like a sapphire in a sexy sequined dress that accentuated her tanned and toned legs, Amelia was a sight to behold as she shimmered her way across the room.

From his vantage point at the bar Tim had watched her, waiting for the familiar surge of excitement to kick in denoting his next conquest; but something else clicked inside him like a light turning on, and for the first time he could ever remember, something besides his healthy libido had him chasing after her. Monogamy wasn't a word in his vocabulary. Neither was love for that matter. But something about Amelia had him seriously wondering what it would be like to be her boyfriend.

After that, things had moved pretty quickly as one date led to another led to Tim and Amelia the couple, surprising nobody more than the commitment-phobe himself.

"No man's an island," she'd tease, sensing his concern about their deepening relationship. Maybe not, but was he really ready to share his strip of the beach?

* * *

"You've been giving your heart away too easily," Minji scolded, as she ferociously rubbed and kneaded the tension from Amelia's knuckles and joints like a baker tormenting her dough. "See," she said pointing accusingly at Amelia's tortured palm, "Your heart line starts between these two fingers." She crushed Amelia's index and middle fingers together and continued, "And it's wavy."

"And wavy means….?" Amelia asked through pain-gritted teeth.

"No good. It means you have lovers but no serious relationships."

"Well now, you know that's not true. Tim and I have been together for a while now."

"Good lover doesn't mean good partner," Minji shrugged and went to work deftly painting each nail with swift, short strokes of color. Amelia thought of Tim and tried to ignore the uneasy feeling growing inside her.

Timothy Smith, aka Adonis, was the man of her dreams and the only man in her life from the moment they met six months ago at the Book Awards dinner; a glittering affair held in the sub-zero ballroom of one of Boston's most magnificent hotels. The party was a veritable Who's Who of publishing gurus and celebrity authors; and Amelia had hovered alone at the bar, keeping warm and passing time by mentally cataloging all the movers and shakers in the room like books on a library shelf.

Holding court in the center of the room were Chadwick and Abby Brown, twin heirs to Brown Books, the oldest and richest publishing house in the U.S. In the corner, single-handedly waging charm warfare on a troop of stylishly-dressed-up beauties, was Monte Monroe, accomplished author, charismatic flirt, and Amelia's own doting uncle.

Amelia owed it all to Monte for getting her here tonight. It was his connections that landed her an internship with Dewes and set the undeclared college student firmly on the path to a career in publishing. Glancing across the bar she spotted her boss, Stuart Gould, chatting with Pashmina Papadakis. She began making her way over to them.

"Excuse me, Miss?" a brandy-smooth voice called, sending a burning thrill up her spine that burst into flame as she turned to gaze into a pair of molten chocolate eyes. "I'm afraid you dropped something back there," the Greek god continued. At her look of confusion, he approached, placing his hands lightly on her shoulders and turning her in the direction she'd just come from. "Do you see that? It's my jaw on the floor. I dropped it there when I saw you."

"Oh my God, that's got to be the worst line I've ever heard," Amelia snorted, turning to look at her offender. "I'm embarrassed for you."

A sardonic smile spread across his exquisite face. "Well, you look like the type of girl who's heard every line in the book. That's the best one I have, so what's one more?"

The rest, as they say, is history. That night, Amelia dined on cheesy pick-up lines and champagne, and fell head over heels in love with a young, ambitious advertising executive named Timothy Smith.

Thinking back to their first date, Amelia recalled introducing him to Rose. "So where's he taking you?" she'd asked, sprawled across Amelia's bed as elegantly as her floral namesake. They were searching for the perfect 'first date' outfit and steadily working their way through Amelia's closet with Amelia holding up multiple options for Rose's expert appraisal. Nine outfits and counting and they still hadn't found 'the one.'

"The Aquarium," Amelia replied nervously. She bit her lip and wished the outfit would just present itself. "Think dim lighting and exotic fishes, very romantic, but a family place, so safe ground for getting to know each other, and interactive, in case, you know, conversation doesn't exactly flow. This guy's put a lot of thought into making sure we have the perfect first date."

"Or maybe he's a serial dater like me and knows all the great date places," Rose quipped. "Or not, I'm just sayin'….." she shrugged catching Amelia's annoyed 'don't mess with me' glare.

"Rose, please. Tim's different. Special."

Rose quietly considered this. No wonder the poor girl was so flustered, she really liked this guy. With newfound understanding, Rose went into action mode. "Okay, move aside and let the pro work her magic."

Planting herself in front of the color-coded wardrobe, Rose draped a comforting arm around Amelia's shoulders and continued in her best 'What Not to Wear' voice. "Now listen and learn, Grasshopper. You want to be impressive but not intimidating, fascinating but not odd, and seductive but not trampy." She winked. "That comes later."

A half hour later, with Rose hovering excitedly behind her, Amelia opened the door and welcomed Tim into their apartment. "Whoa," he breathed, his espresso eyes gazing at her admiringly, "You look amazing." Come to think of it, she felt pretty incredible too, in a black silk dress, soft and clingy in all the right places, a classic strand of pearls, a graduation gift from Francesca, and strappy patent leather sandals.

He leaned in to kiss her hello, his lips warm and soft on her cheek, his nearness and spicy cologne intoxicating. "Tim, this is my friend and roommate, Rose," Amelia introduced them, glancing apologetically at Tim as Rose launched into her customary 'date inquisition.'

Amelia's self-proclaimed wing man since their college days, Rose took her duties to defend and protect her friend very seriously. "I've got your back" she'd pledged to Amelia as they sat in the student union strategizing emergency escape plans for dates gone wrong. True to Rose's word, it had been years since Amelia had dated a guy who hadn't first been interrogated by Rose; and although her judgments were sometimes misguided, she had a pretty good track record for spotting the bad apples.

"So you're going to the Aquarium tonight?" Rose asked rhetorically. "Have you ever been there before? What's your favorite exhibit? Do you like fish? Do you like to eat fish? What's your favorite restaurant?"

"Yes. Yes. The Harbor Seals and what were the rest of your questions?" Tim countered. Amelia watched as he sparred with Rose, noting the amused smile on his chiseled face. His trim fingers combed through his jet black hair, the ends of which just brushed the burgundy collar of a chamois shirt stretched tight across his muscular chest. Perfectly faded designer jeans hugged his athletic legs and a pair of never-been-worn Timberlands completed Tim's lumberjack chic.

"So do you have any logger friends you could set me up with?" Rose asked, eyeing him from head to toe.

"Rose!"

"It's okay," Tim assured her. "Actually she's not completely off base," he turned towards Amelia, his mouth crooked in a sheepish grin. "Would you mind terribly making a quick stop before the Aquarium? The Wilderness Stores' advertising account is up for review and there's a small meet and mingle tonight with some of the corporate execs. I can't even tell you the crimes I committed to score an invitation to the party."

"But it's your first date!"

Amelia shot a grateful look at her wing man, loving Rose for saying what she couldn't.

"I know, I'm sorry the timing couldn't be worse," Tim apologized. "But I promise I'll make it up to you on our next date."

Our next date. Amelia liked the sound of that even though this one had yet to lift-off. "It's fine, no problem," she lied, trying to hide her disappointment. "We'll go schmooze for a little while and then I'll let you buy me dinner afterwards."

With disbelief and disapproval warring across her lovely face, Rose could only stare as Amelia moved quickly out the door blowing a kiss good-bye as she went.

Rose had never forgiven Tim that first misstep or the fact that he had never even tried to redeem himself with her. "I'm not dating Rose," he'd said when Amelia urged him to be more endearing. Hence, six months later, he was still on Rose's probationary shit list.

And six months later, Amelia still had her own doubts. Tim was a great guy, handsome and interesting; they had fun together. She loved him dearly, but enough to spend the rest of her life with him? Even now she still didn't really know Tim, not the way you're supposed to know everything about the person you love. And as long as he continued to keep her at arm's length, it could be a while before that day came.

"I've gotta go," Amelia told Minji, waving her freshly painted nails wildly in the air, and propelling herself out the door. "I'm meeting Tim for dinner."

"See you next week," Minji yelled after her. "Thanks for the tip!"

"You too," Amelia yelled back, wondering which of them was truly the better tipper.

* * *

"Watch it." A strong arm curled around her waist and pulled Amelia safely back to the sidewalk as a taxi cab flew suddenly past her.

"Jesus, I didn't even see him." She turned to her savior and smiled. "Thanks, Superman."

"All in a day's work," sniffed Tim, flexing a well-muscled arm.

"Well, in that case," she asked, batting her long, thick lashes, "can this damsel in distress at least buy you dinner?"

"Now you're talking. All this hero business has made me hungrier than a pitcher in the World Series."

Linking her arm through his, Amelia rolled her eyes as they made their way across the street to Bulls n' Buns.

Settling into a red leather booth for two, they barely glanced at the menu before ordering. "I'll start with a bowl of chowder followed by a Mammoth burger rare, fries on the side and a 20-ounce draft," Tim informed the hovering waitress, handing her his menu and nodding for Amelia to order next.

"That sounds good," Amelia said, handing over her menu as well, "I'll have the same please."

"I've never met another woman who eats like a horse and still looks as good as you do," Tim smirked, leaning across the table to steal a kiss. "How do you do it?"

"If I told you, I'd have to kill you," she quipped, kissing him back, "and what good would that do us?" She ran a freshly polished nail across the flesh of his palm, smiling as he trembled in response. "So speaking of pitchers and the World Series, how was the game last night? Did you have fun?"

"Baseball's not my idea of fun," Tim grimaced, "but try telling that to Ben. Man, he's a pain in the ass. He wouldn't leave my office until I agreed to go with him."

"That's what you call a good friend," Amelia laughed as he squirmed uncomfortably.

"Maybe that's what you call it. I call it blackmail."

"Come again?" she choked on a sip of beer.

"It was a long time ago." He stopped, reluctant to revisit the past but it was even harder to ignore Amelia's prodding. "We were in college. The night before graduation Ben, Chad and I went to a party where someone spiked Chad's drink with a laxative. If it'd been anyone else it wouldn't have been a big deal," Tim shrugged, "but for Chadwick Brown IV it might as well have been arsenic. At least then his dad couldn't kill him when our class president failed to show and give the senior class address. The first C.B. not to speak at commencement since the beginning of time I think."

Amelia was curious. "What happened?"

"Well, his sister Abby gave the speech instead. Then Chad's dad ripped him a new asshole and stuffed it full of guilt about embarrassing his family and disappointing his poor, dead mother."

"He didn't!"

26

"He did. I've gotta hand it to ole' Chad senior. He's a hard ass that can find the soft spot on any living being, especially his own son. Chad adored his mother. When she died during our senior year, he was devastated."

They ate quietly for a moment, lost in their own thoughts until finally Amelia questioned, "So did you do it?"

"Do what?" Tim asked perplexed.

"Did you put the laxative in Chad's drink?"

"What kind of a fool do you think I am?" he scowled, attacking his burger again. "Some people might think Little Lord Fauntleroy is too busy deciding which silver spoon to use to even care what other people do, but not me. Messing with Chad is serious business. He doesn't forgive and he never forgets. I'd rather suffer through a stupid baseball game with Ben than risk the wrath of Chad."

Hiding a smile, Amelia said, "I think it's great. You needed to loosen up a little, have some fun."

"Trust me, I know how to have fun," he said, seductively skimming his thumb across the back of her hand.

"You do?" she asked, feigning wide-eyed innocence.

"Oh yeah." He smiled, causing her heart to skip a beat. She crossed her legs against the tidal wave of sensation growing between them.

He gazed into her eyes, shining pools of lavender mirroring his own excitement, and he felt himself grow hard. Stroking her hand, he imagined her nipple beneath his thumb blossoming like a rosebud from his touch and marveled at the smooth and creamy complexion of her breast. Kissing one and then the other perfect orb, the heat of her skin scorching his lips. Oh, baby.

"Want to play a game with me?" His voice was hoarse but his message was perfectly clear.

"What's it called?" Breathing heavily, Amelia signaled for the check.

"Fuck Me."

Oh my.....

* * *

"Rise and shine, kiddo," Tim said, pulling back the covers and giving a light slap to Amelia's firm bottom. "It's a work day!"

Groaning in denial, she searched frantically for the covers to ward off the chill that was starting to creep over her sleep-warmed skin. "You say that like it's a good thing," she glared.

"Well, it's definitely not bad. In fact, I think it's going to be a great day!"

"And I think you've got problems." Reluctantly Amelia climbed out of bed and followed Tim to the bathroom to brush her teeth while he shaved. "So why is today going to be such a great day?" she asked, feeling perkier with a fresh, clean mouth.

"Remember the Wilderness Stores party we went to?"

"How could I forget?" The event that almost ended their relationship before it began. Despite Tim's promise of a quick 'pitch and go,' it had turned into an all-night networking pow-wow. Well, maybe not all night, but the date part of it at least. At first she didn't mind. Multiple open bars meant everyone had a drink in their hands at all times. Rounds of mouth-watering mini beef wellingtons, crispy bacon-wrapped scallops and a host of other tantalizing hors d'ouevres circled past her frequently enough to threaten dinner later. And watching Tim in action was all the entertainment she needed.

Like a giant cat he had circled the room looking for prey to pounce on with his schmooze and charm; and Amelia had watched with interest as he selectively chose his targets. Only the most powerful people in the room earned his time and attention. He peppered them with questions, laughed politely at their jokes, made sure they had plenty to eat and drink. By the end of the evening, he had bagged himself an invitation to pitch marketing strategies for the Wilderness Stores' brand.

"They're announcing their new agency of record today. Out of six initial agencies, only two are still in the running. Trillingham is one of them," Tim crowed proudly.

"Wow, Babe, that's awesome. I know you really put your heart and soul into those presentations."

He agreed. "It was sort of like a group project in college you know? I burned a lot of midnight oil doing eighty-five percent of the work even though Roger was co-manager on the project. But if," he smiled brightly, "correction when, we get this account, I'm sure my efforts won't be overlooked."

Amelia gave a long slow whistle. "Are we talking about a promotion here?"

Dodging her question, Tim planted a firm kiss upon her lips. "I'm not talking about anything. I'm just saying that I really put myself out there for this account and I think my bosses know that. Now, what've you got going on today?"

"I will have my nose buried in a book today," she announced proudly. "Well, not a book so much as Pashmina's manuscript; my first BIG editorial assignment."

"That's right; I almost forgot," Tim said absently, already thinking of the day ahead. He finished tying his shoe laces and stood up. "Okay, I've gotta go." He kissed the tip of her nose and walked to the bedroom door. "Have fun with your manuscript and keep your fingers crossed for me."

Amelia finished dressing and made her way to the kitchen where Ben waited with her favorite caffeinated beverage, Diet Coke. "The early bird said you were here before he dashed off to catch the worm," Ben said dryly, answering her unasked question. "Personally, I think pre-dawn protein is highly overrated."

Amelia laughed, nodding her agreement. "I'm with you. I need real food before I dig into my day. Do you have any Pop-Tarts?"

CHAPTER THREE

The sound of seagulls and crashing waves filled the room as Amelia's cell phone rang. Sitting at her desk, she was thoroughly enjoying the advance peek at Pashmina's manuscript, furiously filling a notebook with line edits and proofing questions. She was feeling more and more like a real editor by the minute. Man, she loved this job.

The ocean sounds emanating from her phone persisted, urging her to answer it.

"Hello?"

"Hey." Tim sounded like a flat tire.

Amelia's good mood vanished. She felt suddenly nervous but forced herself to sound normal. "Hey, yourself, what's new?"

"Not much, except we got the Wilderness Stores' account."

Doing a little chair dance Amelia squealed into the phone. "Babe, that's so awesome! That's great! It's fantastic! Congratulations." Closing her eyes she mouthed a heartfelt "Thank you." Life was good for both of them right now.

"How about I come over tonight and cook you a special celebratory dinner? Whatever you want: steak, lobster, pasta. You name it, I'll make it; cause that's the kind of fabulous girlfriend I am."

Deafening silence met her ears.

"Tim?"

"Yeah, I'm here. Hey listen, I'll have to take a rain check on dinner. There's an agency high-five happening tonight and the whole account team needs to be there. Sorry."

"Of course, sure, I understand," she said, completely underwhelmed by his enthusiasm. "Whenever you want."

"Okay, thanks. Listen, I've gotta go now. I just wanted to let you know about the account. I'll call you tomorrow."

Something was wrong. Amelia knew it. She had felt this way with him before. Shortly after they met, she had invited him to go with her to South Carolina to visit her mom. She knew it was a bold move so early in their relationship, but she was falling hard and fast for Tim, and she needed the one person who knew her better than anybody to tell her if she was headed for a crash landing or soft ground.

"Sounds to me like someone needs some girl time with her Mom," Tim declined, as they relaxed on her couch, legs entwined, Amelia's head resting on his chest. "I'd just be in the way."

Unwilling to let it go, she had tried her best to coax him. "I probably haven't painted the best picture of my mom, but trust me, she's no different from yours. She loves her kid, and at the end of the day all she wants is for me to be happy and safe." Raising her head, she kissed him lightly on the lips. "She's dying to meet the guy who makes me feel that way."

But no amount of sweet-talking or seduction had changed Tim's mind. Later, on her way to South Carolina alone, as the cloud cover cleared and the plane ascended into open skies, she had played their conversation over and over in her head. Tim was adamant he wouldn't go, but not for the reason she thought. "C'mon, Amelia," he'd huffed, exasperated, threading his hands through his hair. "Do you honestly think I'm afraid to meet your mother, the woman who gave me you?"

Amelia had melted of course, what girl wouldn't? And she accepted his refusal without further explanation. But she never stopped feeling like there was more to the story.

"Is everything alright, Babe?" She wanted to know. "You sound.….off."

"Everything's fine. Just great."

His annoyance was obvious, so she decided to cut him some slack and end the call. "Well, have a good time tonight. I love you and I'll talk to you tomorrow."

*   *   *

The phone stuck in his hand like glue, a silent reminder of unfinished business. Why didn't you tell her? Tim's conscious prodded. I told her what she needed to know. I told her what I could. But you didn't tell her everything did you?

Probably because he still couldn't believe it himself. How could he not get a promotion for bringing in the Wilderness Stores' account? Even worse, how did Roger get it? Certainly not by kissing every power ass that mattered, and definitely not by working his ass off like Tim had. He slammed his empty hand on the desk, the harsh sting staining his palm red. It just wasn't fair.

Tim smiled bitterly. No surprise there. Fair was not how he would describe his life, but this was no time for a pity party. It was time to go flash his mega-watt smile, slap a few shoulders, and congratulate the man of the hour on his new 14th floor digs. "I hear the air's pretty thin up there," he'd joke, "watch out for altitude sickness." And everyone would laugh, except Tim of course. He didn't find it funny at all.

*   *   *

"Hey," Ben yawned the next morning, taking a stool at the breakfast bar where Tim sat reading the morning newspaper, a half-eaten bowl of cereal in front of him. "You going to finish that?" he asked hungrily, eyeing the milk-sodden flakes.

"There's a full box of cereal in the cupboard. Why don't you get your own breakfast?" Ben frowned as his growling stomach echoed the gruffness of Tim's voice. Tearing his gaze from the object of his desire, he turned to study his roommate more closely. Something was off. Instead of his usual conservative chic, Tim was sporting more of a casual Friday look, and it was only Wednesday. He was staring intently at the paper spread in front of him like it might get up and walk away, but Ben could tell he wasn't reading it. And he had restless finger syndrome, fidgeting with the medallion around his neck, turning it over and over again as if it could somehow help.

"You clearly have no intention of finishing that," Ben nodded towards the bowl, "so why can't I have it?"

"Jesus, everything's a federal case with you, isn't it?" Tim snarled, shoving the bowl towards Ben. "Just take it."

"Thanks." Smiling brightly, Ben scooped a hefty spoonful of mush into his mouth. He hadn't seen Tim this pissed off in a long time. Ben knew it would take every ounce of tact and skill he had to calm Tim down. Better fuel up before trying to find out what had his roommate's panties in a twist this time.

With studied interest, Tim watched as Ben munched his breakfast, happy and relaxed despite the impending pressures of the work day ahead. How many mornings like this one had they shared over the years, bickering like an old married couple with nothing better to do than annoy the hell out of each other? Too many probably, but Ben had been his first roommate in college and Tim could never be bothered to find anyone else to live with after that.

Their senior year, Ben had invited Chad to live with them in a small apartment barely big enough for two, but rent enough for three. "You're shitting me," Tim said when Ben told him about their new roommate. "What the hell? That guy's got enough money to live in the Taj Mahal if he wanted to. What'd you ask him to live with us for?"

"Because we could use the extra money, and because he's a good guy," Ben explained, adding softly, "If you gave him a chance, you'd know that."

"Hmmph." Tim snorted. "Chadwick Brown IV's had more chances than anybody, thank you. And more privileges, too. That poor little rich boy doesn't need any help from us. Besides, what could we possibly give him that he doesn't already have?"

"Friends," said Ben and he laughed as Tim's mouth dropped open. "Yeah, believe it or not, all the money in the world won't buy happiness or friends and Chad doesn't have a lot of either." So, despite Tim's wishes, Chad had moved in. For Ben's sake, Tim had made a reluctant effort to befriend the guy preordained to one day spearhead one of the greatest publishing empires in the country.

Unlike Chad, familial destiny was not something either Ben or Tim had going for them. When they met, Tim had assumed that Bennington Grey was also the product of a long and distinguished heritage. He quickly realized that Ben, the middle child of a bank manager and a school teacher, was a nondescript, self-motivated go-getter like himself. Equal parts brain and charisma, Ben was a campus favorite among faculty and students. With his enviable looks and athletic prowess, the guy had legions of both women and men vying for his attention.

To hear Ben tell it, his inherent talent for lawyering became apparent early in life when he was routinely forced to mediate arguments and negotiate settlements between his older and younger sisters. Thanks to them, he had learned the value of astute listening, the power of carefully chosen words, and the importance of compassion, all of which helped him to develop a commanding triumvirate of skills that set him apart from the pack. In a city full of legal eagles, Ben was a rising star attorney.

Tim sighed. They were quite the trio: Mr. Money, Mr. Popularity, and Mr. Loser. The sound of Ben's spoon scraping the now empty bowl brought Tim back to the present. "Why don't you just lick it clean?" he growled.

"Testy, testy, somebody got up on the wrong side of the bed this morning. Or did Amelia kick your sorry ass out?" Ben teased.

"Shut the fuck up," Tim scowled. "She's not even here."

Startled, Ben raised his hands against the sudden outburst and tried to apologize. "Whoa, buddy, I was just joking." Silence settled between them. A sudden thought made Ben shift a safe distance away. "Is everything okay with you two?"

"We're fine." Tim thought about Amelia blossoming in her new role at Dewes. Was it providence or fate that dropped Pashmina in her lap? It didn't even matter. Just add Miss Lucky to the list.

"So what's the problem then? You look mad enough to commit murder."

"More like hari kari but that's not a bad idea."

"You lost me."

"We won the Wilderness Stores' account," Tim paused, holding up a hand, "but before you get all excited, I didn't get a promotion to go along with it."

Ben paused from rinsing his bowl at the sink. "Well that sucks, but at least you get credit for bringing in the account. That has to count for something, if not now, then in the future."

"And that's exactly what I thought when the president himself came to congratulate me on a job well done and 'for my efforts above and beyond' " Tim air quoted. "Then he proceeded to tell me that Roger, my dick-head

36

project co-manager, was being promoted to Vice President of the consumer division, and I'd have full ownership of the new account."

Ben was confused. "Full ownership, that's good isn't it?"

"It's bullshit." Tim was on a tear. "I had full ownership of the entire pitch project because Roger didn't do a fucking thing except agree with my ideas and leave me to build the presentation by myself. He's the fucking head of Creative but I was the one who worked with his team to craft a creative strategy. He didn't even come up with one damn story board. So is it good that he's promoted to overseeing an entire division while I stay in the trenches watching over one little account? Not in my book."

The men fell silent, Tim staring at his clenched hands as Ben wiped his with a dish towel. Reclaiming his seat at the breakfast bar, Ben spoke quietly. "I'm sorry, buddy." He stopped then started again. "I know it blows, but is it really the end of the world? I mean nobody died or anything right?" When Tim didn't respond, Ben asked, "What did Amelia say about it?"

Tim's head dipped low and Ben understood. "I don't get it," he said shaking his head. "She's your girlfriend, for Christ's sake. Why wouldn't you tell her?"

"Maybe I don't want to. Did that ever occur to you?" Tim's eyes blazed. "Just because we're in a relationship doesn't mean she's entitled to know everything about me."

"Entitled?" Ben couldn't believe his ears. "You think telling Amelia you didn't get a promotion makes her entitled? Wow, that's pretty arrogant, even for you!"

"What's that supposed to mean?"

"It means even a self-centered bastard like you should know when someone's on your side. Can't you see she's in love with you?"

"And that's exactly why I didn't tell her," Tim snapped, "Nobody loves a loser." Grabbing the paper, he shook it open with a vengeance. "I'm done with this conversation."

Ben sat quietly staring at the newspaper now serving as a barrier between them, thinking as the minutes passed. After a while, he reached up and gently pulled the pages down until they were eye-to-eye.

"Maybe it's time to go to another agency," he suggested. "It's always easier to command more status and more money as a new blood than a loyal soldier. Or maybe you should leave the agency world altogether, go corporate and look for an in-house position. Don't you handle the advertising for Amelia's company?"

Tim nodded.

"So you know something about marketing and publishing. Now all you need is a contact." Grinning and rubbing a thumb across his chin, Ben pretended to think, "Do we know anyone you can call?"

Throwing the folded paper on the counter, Tim rolled his eyes. "Why would Chad want to help me?" he asked.

Sobered by the question, Ben gave an earnest reply, "Because that's what friends do."

Wishing he could share Ben's conviction, Tim grudgingly conceded, "All right, I'll think about it."

CHAPTER FOUR

Pashmina stared mindlessly out the living room window of her
Beacon Hill home, watching her neighbor struggle to remove a decorative
fruit wreath from her front door before it succumbed to the powerful forces
of the summer storm shrieking outside. Too late, Mrs. Mackenzie could only
watch as the gale-like wind ripped demonically through the plastic and wire
accessory, sending lemons and peaches hurtling down the cobblestone street.
Refusing to surrender, she inhaled deeply, wrestling the tattered decoration
off its hook and into the safety of her home as Pashmina silently cheered.

Turning away from the window, Pashmina settled comfortably on
her gold patterned couch. The cozy warmth of the crackling fire enveloped
her like a soft blanket covering a sleeping child. It was a moderate storm as
these things go, but a storm just the same, and the New England idiom 'if you
don't like the weather, wait a minute it'll change,' came to mind.

On the sofa table behind her, a wine decanter beckoned, and she
poured herself a glass, sighing contentedly as the ruby elixir turned her tired
muscles molten. After months of stressful preparation, the book was in
Amelia's hands now; and Pashmina could finally relax. Grateful for the
respite, she closed her eyes and sank deep into the sofa cushions. A flurry of
memories scurried through her mind like the fruits from Mrs. Mackenzie's
wreath, some sweet, others not so much.

It had happened a year ago. Pashmina had just wrapped another
book tour and was returning to Greece for her first visit home in a long time.
She felt the excitement bubbling inside her before the plane even left New

York, eager to see her parents, her brothers and their expanding families. How many nieces and nephews now? Sometimes she lost count. And, of course, she thought about Harry.

Thirty years ago, Harry Lynch was a handsome, young midshipman in the Royal Navy with hair the color of burnished copper and eyes as green as the Emerald Isle of his ancestors. Harry was sweet and funny and kind, and for a fleeting moment, he was the husband she adored. Then just as quickly, her marriage was over. "It's the right thing to do," he had said and no amount of pleading or crying had earned her any further explanation.

Even now her heart still ached for a life that might have been, but inexplicably never was. Harry had moved on, re-married, raised a family and five years ago lost a battle with cancer. Despite the years and distance between them, her love for him had never waned and his death had hit her hard.

Burrowing deeper into the couch, she allowed the memories of that trip to Greece to continue to wash over her.

One afternoon, overwhelmed by the cacophony of family reunion noise and chaos, Pashmina sought refuge in the quiet comfort of a familiar café. The warm sun and soothing murmur of nearby conversations had her nearly dozing when a man slid suddenly into the empty seat across from her, startling her wide awake.

He had a few more lines on his perpetually tanned face and his once thick brown hair was now a mop of soft steel curls that tumbled wildly on his neck, but his roguish smile and shining eyes like crystal blue pools were just as she remembered them. She would have known him anywhere. "You're late," she smiled at George, "about twenty-nine years late, in fact."

"Twenty-eight years, six months, and three days actually," he corrected Pashmina, casually drinking from the tea cup in front of her. His bright expression dimmed and he waved the waiter over, "Ouzo, please, and plenty of it."

Pashmina laughed, secretly grateful for the fortifying liquid. So many years had passed since they had last seen each other, what must she look like to him now? "Am I so scary you need liquid courage to face me?"

"On the contrary, Pashmina, you're exactly as I remember you, lovelier than ever." George's eyes glowed like sapphires and he shrugged, uncharacteristically shy, "but after all this time, nerves of steel would be useful right now." Reaching across the table, he grasped her hand firmly in his. "How are you?"

His skin was rough, calloused but warm, and Pashmina relaxed immediately, the way she used to whenever he touched her. Blushing, she pulled the traitorous hand into the solitary confinement of her lap where it twitched, lonely and alone, much like she'd been when George Levendakis entered her life.

Pashmina had only been married for nine months, with Harry away at sea for the last two, when she first met George at a lecture for novice writers. He was an investigative journalist for the Athens daily newspaper, and one of four panelists who spoke about the challenges of becoming a proficient and published author, the very thing Pashmina dreamed of becoming. Engaging and funny and knowledgeable, George was a standout panelist; and she had sought him out at the post-lecture coffee hour.

She found him easily, a lone figure in the midst of a growing group of giggling girls. No surprise there, Mr. Levendakis was brilliant and gorgeous, and Pashmina didn't have a prayer of breaking through the ever-expanding estrogen barrier surrounding him. Feeling thwarted and disappointed she moved to leave when a familiar voice called out to her.

"Darling, there you are!"

Pashmina turned slightly to see the crowd parting like the Red Sea and George crossing through it directly toward her. "I'm so glad you could make it. It's lovely to see you," he exclaimed, grinning from ear-to-ear. Taking hold of her elbow, he guided her toward the coffee station, his lips whispering conspiratorially against her ear, "Save me, please."

"I don't understand," she started, overwhelmingly conscious of her tingling ear. "How can I help you, Mr. Levendakis?"

"Call me George, please, and believe me, you've already done more than you know." He winked, flirtatious, but mischievous as a little boy which made Pashmina laugh.

"Well, I'm not sure what I've done to make you so happy, but it was my pleasure," she said, smiling. "It's the least I can do to thank you for the inspiring talk you gave tonight."

"I'm glad you enjoyed it." Smiling warmly in return, his eyes roamed the contours of her beautiful face. "But you have me at a disadvantage, Ms.?"

"Mrs.," she corrected, wondering if she had only imagined his eyes dimming at the assertion. "Pashmina Papadakis, I mean Lynch." Blushing lightly she explained, "I haven't been married very long."

"Timing's never been my strong suit," George lamented, mesmerized by the growing blush heating Pashmina's soft cheeks into blossoming roses and he felt his own blood warm in response. "But fate must have brought us together for a reason, don't you think?"

George's voice poured over her like satin, silky and smooth, and Pashmina struggled to breathe. A wayward coffee cup smashed nearby, providing a welcome distraction as she mentally pulled herself together. "I'm sure fate had nothing to do with it, Mr., I mean, George," she corrected herself. "We make our own decisions, our own choices. For example, I chose to come here tonight."

With a slight bow, he conceded her point. "And I decided I couldn't let the gorgeous woman sitting in the fourth row, fifth seat from the left leave before I knew her name," he teased.

Trapped in his piercing blue gaze, Pashmina was nervous. She should leave, that much she knew, but she was captivated. And flattered. Attempting to bring the conversation back to safer ground, she inquired, "You're a newspaper reporter. Are you also a novelist?" George's handsome mouth lifted in a crooked smile, making her wonder what it would be like to kiss those full masculine lips.

"Not yet," he answered, pulling her gaze back to his, "but one day I will be. I just need inspiration and the right story." Still smiling, he pressed his lips to her hand, "the good news is my inspiration just arrived, and I'm sure the rest can't be far behind."

Pashmina's throat was dry and her knees felt like jelly. Get a grip; you're a married woman! She thought about Harry; only a few more months and he would be home. Then finally they could start building a life together with a home of their own and children. "We'll have so many babies we'll have our own football team," he'd crowed, pulling her close for an impassioned kiss, "or at least we'll have fun trying!"

She sighed. Her heart happily belonged to Harry; she just wanted him home, desperately. In the meantime, this naval wife would put her heart into other passionate pursuits. Since she was a little girl, she had kept a diary, loving the feel of the pen in her hand, the way it moved at her command, putting thoughts and feelings on paper. But as she had grown older, the girlish musings of her journal entries got old, too, and a new dream was born.

"Are you an author?" George's question interrupted Pashmina's thoughts.

"Trying to be," she admitted, slightly embarrassed. "I mean, I've written a few short stories, but nothing that would knock your socks off, and I've never had anything published."

"Writing is the hardest thing about being an author, you know." Pashmina shot George a look of annoyance and he laughed. "I'm serious. Putting your ideas into words that other people connect with is an enormous challenge, but if you're successful, there's no greater honor." Sweeping his hand through the air he painted a picture, "Just imagine, millions of people waiting to get their hands on your book, the next great novel from Pashmina Papadakis."

"Lynch," she said dreamily, relishing the image he created, "the next great novel by Pashmina Lynch."

George frowned. "Not quite the same ring to it, but …" He was standing so close he could almost hear her silent wish, and suddenly he wanted nothing more than to make it happen. Beneath that pure feminine exterior was an ambitious young woman eager to break out, but not sure how. Maybe he was crazy, he had only just met her and he didn't really know anything about her. It wasn't a habit of his to help other people, even beautiful women like Pashmina, but right now making her dreams come true was the only thing he wanted to do.

Excited, he grabbed her hands. "Pashmina, let me help you. I can coach you. I can introduce you to people in publishing. We can work together, you on your book and me on mine. Please, just say 'yes'."

He pleaded with her like a puppy dog begging for a treat and Pashmina laughed, delighted. George Levendakis, the practiced investigative writer so skilled he was being hailed as the next Carl Bernstein, wanted to work with her! Thank you, guardian angel.

Their 'tutoring' sessions began that night as they talked over coffee. In the following months they met several times a week to discuss writing processes, create plot outlines, and of course to write, she at her typewriter, George tapping away next to her on his. At times their discussions were heated, both of them having their own strong opinions on things, and other times they wrote in companionable silence; but always, Pashmina was happy reveling in the friendship they shared. In fact, she was depending on it more and more every day to fill the void caused by Harry's prolonged absence.

In contrast to the emptiness around her, George was vibrant and warm; he believed in her, believed that she could be a great writer, and he made her feel beautiful with his silly incessant professions of desire. She felt cherished; George loved her and she was deeply fond of him. What woman wouldn't be? He was charming and funny, attentive and attractive, and he pursued her relentlessly until she couldn't resist him any longer.

In retrospect, she supposed their affair was inevitable. That's what happens when an ardently amorous man and an infatuated young woman jump off a cliff together. It was fast and furious and passionate and it was wrong. Pashmina knew it and was consumed with guilt and remorse. George was a terrific guy, but Harry was her husband; he was the one she wanted to share her life with. The connection between her and George had to end.

Saying goodbye to George wasn't the hardest thing she would ever have to do, but it hadn't been easy, especially since George disagreed vehemently, alternately pleading and arguing with her not to destroy their relationship. "Don't do this, Pashmina," he begged, "We have something other people only dream of."

But if she had had any doubts, Harry's homecoming soon after was all she needed to set her straight and remind her how much she loved her husband. And he loved her too. Pashmina had seen it shining brightly in Harry's eyes dark with passion. She had felt it in the tenderness of his kisses and the gentleness of his hands as they skimmed over her warm, bare skin, reacquainting themselves with the curves and valleys of her body. Pashmina was in heaven.

Until Harry left suddenly for no reason, without any explanation, and the bottom fell out of her happy little world. What the hell happened? Mystified, she tried to make sense of it all, futilely begging Harry to talk to her and seeking comfort from her mother. "You can't force a heart to change the way it feels, Sweetheart. Let him go," her mother urged, stroking Pashmina's long, dark hair as her daughter sobbed in her arms. "Let him go and the pain will go too. In time."

Praying for time to fly and Harry to come back, Pashmina was less than enthused when George's note arrived asking her to meet him at a local cafe. *'It's important, Pashmina, a matter of life or death. Please come.'* George always did have a flare for the dramatic. She smiled slightly, wondering what could be so imperative and debated the wisdom of going at all. The last thing she wanted was to fuel any false hopes of their getting back together.

To her surprise, though, it was George who didn't show. Pashmina waited for him well past their appointed meeting time. Annoyed, she was getting ready to pack it in when a messenger approached her table with a large manila envelope and a letter addressed to her:

Dearest Pashmina,

Forgive me. I promise you that nothing short of extreme circumstances would have kept me from you today and in fact the situation is dire. I have to go away for a while. I'm not sure where or for how long. I'm afraid that's all I can tell you without putting you in danger as well. Until I can return to you, I'm entrusting my heart and this package to your precious and infinite care. Please guard them well and wait for me.

Forever yours,

George

And just like that, both men in her life were gone and Pashmina surrendered, finally giving in to the grief and despair that followed her everywhere. Existing, but not living, she wandered through the days, listless, without purpose, conserving all her remaining energy until the hurt slowly scabbed over and she could breathe without screaming. After a while, the fog began to lift, and gradually she began to feel more like herself again, young and strong. And pregnant.

"What's that for?" she snorted as Sofie shoved a pregnancy stick in her hand. Her dearest friend in the world, Sofie was the only living person who knew about her and George.

"Probably nothing," she shrugged, "but maybe something."

Pashmina was stunned. "You think I'm pregnant?" A mental calendar flipped through her head as she tried to recall her last period. Admittedly, the throes of depression hadn't been kind to her body, melting away too many pounds, robbing the luster from her skin and hair; she had barely noticed the absence of her natural cycle. "Impossible." Crossing her arms defiantly, Pashmina winced as they rubbed against her full and tender breasts. Uh oh.

Thrilled at first, her initial joy was quickly squelched by the certainty that George was the father; and a father missing in action at that. Even if she wanted to tell him, she had no idea where he was or how to find him. If only it was Harry's baby, then everything would be right again; she would go to him and they would live happily ever after, but dreaming didn't change the facts. She would never try to pass another man's baby off as Harry's. She couldn't do that to him, but she couldn't live without him either.

Ultimately it was Sofie who came up with the solution to all of Pashmina's problems. "You need to leave Greece, Pashmina. Go somewhere no one knows you and have the baby. People are always looking to adopt newborns, you won't have any problem finding a good home for yours, and then you'll be free to go after Harry.

Pashmina was uncertain. "It sounds so simple."

But Sofie was confident. "We'll have to come up with something to tell your mother and your family, but I'll help you," she promised.

Pashmina was overwhelmed with the guilt of lying to her family, but she knew that Sofie was right, and she followed her friend's advice. Only once had she briefly looked back on her former life, when she discovered the unopened manila envelope from George carelessly shoved into one of the many unpacked moving boxes.

It appeared to be a manuscript. Scanning the pages of neatly typed words, Pashmina had quickly recognized his methodical style of writing, laying out the facts word by word, chapter upon chapter, like a builder erecting a skyscraper; a style as different from her own imaginative chaos as night from day. And as Pashmina read his story, she understood why he had left it in her possession. It was unequivocally the best thing he had ever written, and undeniably the greatest secret he could never tell. By entrusting her with the manuscript, George had placed his life and his future completely in her hands.

For twenty-nine years she had kept his secret buried deep amongst her affection and concern for him, forbidding herself to even think of it again, until today. Now sitting here in the same café where they were to have met decades earlier, the truth came rushing back.

"I take it, it's safe for you to be here now?" she asked, one eyebrow arched questioningly.

George laughed. "And you're still not one to beat around the bush are you? Does this mean you read my manuscript? What do you think of it?"

Without hesitation she answered, "It's your best work yet and you know it. But, George, you know you can never publish it without incriminating yourself," she warned, concerned for her friend.

"Ironic isn't it? I finally got my story and I'll never be able to tell it."
He raised his glass, drinking deeply under Pashmina's thoughtful gaze. Was it
disappointment or sadness or something else shading his handsome face?

"Where have you been all this time? What have you been doing?" she
asked, her own voice heavy and sad.

He smiled. "Don't feel bad for me, Pashmina. I've had a good life. At
first I traveled a lot, always moving, afraid the past would catch up with me.
But eventually I came home, back to Greece. I've been living in Cronilys ever
since."

"Are you still writing?" she asked curious.

"Not really, I'm a fisherman now." He held up his calloused hands
for her inspection. "I use my hands to haul nets and catch fish instead of
tapping keys on a typewriter or a computer. That's what you use, isn't it?"

Pashmina nodded before protesting, "But how could you stop
writing? It was your passion."

"No, Pashmina, it was my job. You were my passion," he said simply,
"From the day we met, and every day after, you were all I ever wanted."

He paused, letting his words sink in, and waited for her to react.
Taking her silence as a good sign, he pressed on. "I've spent the past twenty-
nine years dreaming of the day we'd be together again. As soon as I thought it
was safe all I wanted was to come find you." He gazed at her with pride. "By
then, of course, you were a famous author, Pashmina Papadakis, and I was
just a hardworking fisherman. What kind of a life could I offer you? But now
here we are, both visitors at the same time and place, and I think fate must be
telling us something, don't you?"

She waved her hand dismissively. "You know I don't believe in that."

"Right, I'd forgotten." He shook his head ruefully. "We make our
own choices and let the chips fall where they may." Silence fell between them
as he studied her intently. Time had been generous to Pashmina, changing the

naive innocent of his memories into a bold and confident woman of the world, but he suspected the two still had much in common.

A broad smile lit his face like the sun coming from behind a cloud. "I choose you, Pashmina. Say the word and we can still have our happy ending."

"Careful what you wish for, George," she warned, trying to keep things lighthearted, "I'm a diva now, you know."

"I'm serious, Pashmina. I know we can't go back but we can start again."

"There's been no 'we' for a long time, George," she said, wary of where this was headed. "Harry was the only one for me; he always was. I told you that."

"You did," he agreed. "But then he left you, and it was supposed to be our time, our chance to be happy. That's what I was going to tell you before everything blew up."

It was as if he hadn't spoken. "Harry's gone, you know, he died a few years ago."

The turn in conversation was getting to him, even as George tried his best to comfort her. "I'm sorry, Pashmina, he was a good man, an admirable one. I know he only wanted what was best for you."

"That's what I used to think," she scoffed, "but an admirable man would never just up and leave his wife." Love and pain cast delicate shadows across her face causing her lips to quiver and her eyes to glow with unshed tears. In George's eyes, she had never looked more beautiful or vulnerable. It was time to come clean.

"I met him, once," he said, instantly grabbing her attention. No going back now. He took a deep breath and continued, "You'd just broken up with me, and I was beside myself because I knew you were making a terrible mistake. We were perfect for each other. So I told him about us, how much we loved each other, how good we were together, and the whole time I

50

prayed he would do the right thing and let you go. That's why I think Harry is an honorable man. He put your needs above his own. Your happiness came first with him."

Understanding dawned slowly but surely as Pashmina tried to make sense of what he was saying. My God, what had George done? "You told Harry about us?" Nausea woke inside her. "Why? Why would you do that to me?"

"It's the right thing to do." She couldn't believe Harry would have agreed, but obviously, George had convinced him. Pashmina had lost the love of her life and her marriage because of George. She had trusted him, cared about him, carried his child. Bile rose in her throat at the thought.

After the baby was born Pashmina had almost refused to let it go, just one look and she had fallen completely in love. But she was scared. What did she know about being a mother and how could she possibly live without Harry? Adoption was the best option for both of them.

Or so she had thought until she finally saw Harry again, a few months later. Then she wondered if she had made the right choice after all. Harry was engaged. He was going to marry his childhood sweetheart. "She's a wonderful girl, lovely and kind," he told Pashmina in a voice so tender it nearly broke her heart. "But not as strong as you, Pashmina. She needs me."

She needs me. If his words hadn't hurt so much, they would have been funny. But there was nothing at all humorous about her situation. Harry was lost to her. George was gone. Her baby was gone. Just me, myself, and I, she thought with steely resolve. And that's how it had been ever since.

"Pashmina?" George was looking at her, concern barely masking his happy expression. "We should be celebrating our reunion, not mourning the past."

She stared at him blankly. For so many years she had struggled to manage the past, ignore the pain of loss and her own costly mistakes. And for what? The past was all a lie, anyway. What if she had told Harry the truth back then, begged for his forgiveness, and convinced him her love was real, would things have turned out differently? Maybe, maybe not, but thanks to George, she would never know.

"You bastard!" Pashmina snarled, slapping away his hands reaching out to calm her. "Get away from me! You ruined my life, and now you want me to be happy about it?"

Pashmina's chest heaved as hot tears spilled onto her cheeks, and she could feel the curious stares of the other patrons judging her. Fuck them. She didn't care.

"You had no right, George." Barely able to look at him, she stood to leave.

"Pashmina, wait."

"For what, so you can hurt me some more? I don't think so." But there was something she needed to know. "Just tell me one thing. If you had met me here that day, would you have told me the truth about Harry then?"

She waited for him to answer, a cocoon of quiet surrounding them, blocking out everything and everyone except the two of them. Their eyes met and locked, hard granite to icy steel.

"No," he said shattering the silence.

Pashmina tilted her head, as if hearing sound for the first time, and saw life happening all around her; a group of teenage girls was preening and giggling trying to catch the attention of a group of young men, a mother pushed a stroller, protectively tucking a blanket around her infant as she went, an elderly couple bowed and bent with age held hands as they walked, their movements synchronized like two dancers who've waltzed together a lifetime.

Pashmina shook her head sadly, sending cob-webbed memories and futile wishes scattering. So much time wasted pining for a man she had lost, a man she would never have again, thanks to George. But no more; she was done.

"Wrong answer," Pashmina replied, stepping onto the crowded sidewalk where the flow of people swept her away from the misery of the cafe, away from George, away from his anguished gaze that continued to burn long after she was out of sight.

* * *

For some time after that fateful meeting and George's full disclosure, Pashmina had lived in a mind-numbing state of nothingness. In less than five minutes, life as she thought she knew it had been turned upside down, leaving her hanging suspended, an emotional wreck and a creative cripple.

He had once claimed that timing wasn't his strong suit, but George had hit the mark perfectly this time. With pressing deadlines bearing down on her, Pashmina was stuck, unable to write a word, paralyzed by his confession. Lethargic, apathetic, and void of her usual ability to write at will, she struggled, half-heartedly chipping away at the mental block impeding her writing while trying to think of another way around it.

The evenings were the hardest. Anxious and uneasy, she was desperate for relief from consciousness. Fighting to get some sleep one night, she had reached into her night table drawer for a sedative and found something else buried under the pile of tissues, notepads, and reading glasses that lived there. George's manuscript weighed heavy in her hands. She pulled the dusty manila folder from the drawer and eyed it suspiciously.

It won't bite you, silly girl. It's just a manuscript you read a long time ago. Too long ago to remember?

Turning the folder over and raising the unsealed flap, Pashmina let the bound pages glide easily out of their protective sleeve and began to read. Maybe a good bedtime story was all she needed.

* * *

Pasmina woke to the sound of logs crackling in the fireplace. Reaching for her glass of wine, she sipped, washing away the bitter taste of her dreams. Just like that. And soon, she'd be rid of George, for good. Just like that. With Amelia's help, she would see to it.

CHAPTER FIVE

George stepped easily over the heavy rope neatly coiled on the dock, the warmth of the early morning sun already heating his skin, and the cool sea air filling his lungs. Early as it was, the village of Cronilys was a bustle of activity as fishermen crowded the docks preparing their boats for a full day of baiting and netting.

"George!" someone yelled, and he turned, squinting against the sun to see who it was.

"What is it, Vasily?" he called, instantly recognizing the short, squat captain of the *Cerilia* fishing boat. As round as he was tall, good natured Vasily was often the butt of many jokes, but no one was more respected on these docks than him. George counted himself lucky to be one of Vasily's crew.

"Grab those buckets of bait and bring them to the front of the boat. We need to take off in the next half hour if we're going to lead the fleet."

George smiled. "Okay, boss. I'll be right there. Just need to grab some tobacco at the Fish Stand. Do you need anything?"

"Get me some too, will you?"

With a wave to Vasily, George headed down the dock towards a small merchant's market called The Fish Stand. Invaluable to those who worked the docks, it had all the things fishermen needed: cigarettes, cold drinks and snacks, not to mention gossip. Once, a long time ago, George had asked why the shop didn't carry newspapers. "What do you need a paper for?" the shop keeper had asked. "Anything you need to know you can find out right here at The Fish Stand."

Chuckling at the memory, George grabbed two packages of chewing tobacco and gave a quick scan of the worn shelves to see if there was anything else he needed.

"Thank you for the fish, Cosmos." A woman's lilting voice sounded pleasantly from the front of the store as George approached the counter. "I'll see you again soon," she promised. Lifting a paper bag filled with her purchases, the woman turned to leave and came eye-to-eye with George standing directly behind her.

Her eyes grew wide as she stared into the baby blues gazing calmly back at her. With casual interest, George let his eyes stray from her face, panning the length of her trim form and back again. She was middle-aged, wearing a blue sundress and leather sandals, her dark hair piled on top of her head. Looking slightly flustered, she gave a nervous smile and moved towards the exit.

"Wait, please," he asked, halting her in her tracks. She looked so familiar. "Have we met before?"

She nodded, resigned. "Yes, George, we've met. I'm Sofie Anastas."

Recognition dawned as he remembered Pashmina's friend. The only person he had ever met from Pashmina's other life. "Why don't you introduce me to any of your friends, your family," he had asked once, eliciting such a look of fear and horror that he had never asked again. If hiding was the only way he could have Pashmina, he would just have to live with it.

"Sofie, of course," he said with a smile, gently guiding her out of the shop and earshot of the gossip mongers inside. "How are you? You're looking well."

"Thanks, so are you. I forgot Pashmina said you're a fisherman now."

His ears perked up at the familiar name. "You've spoken to her?"

"Now and then," she shrugged nonchalantly. "Not as much as we'd like, but we're all busy, you know?" She stared at him unabashed. Pashmina was right, he had aged well, but he was still trouble. Pursing her lips, she shook her head slightly. "She also said you ruined her life and she hopes she never sees you again."

George winced. Sofie hadn't mellowed at all over the years. Her tongue was as bold and blunt as ever. "Mm hmm, I believe that," he agreed, "typical Pashmina, never taking any responsibility for her own actions."

"Excuse me?" Sofie sputtered. "Pashmina's one of the most responsible people I know. She had to be to clean up the mess you left her in."

George's blood began to boil. It took two to tango, didn't it? All he had done was fight for the woman he loved. "So I'm the bad guy for telling her husband about us? I'm so sick and tired of hearing that shit, Sofie. Pashmina needs to grow up. She was the married one. Don't you think it was her responsibility to tell him?"

"Oh, George, you always did think things were simple." But not for Pashmina. Even Sofie had wondered if they were doing the right thing sending her away from everything she knew and loved. Pashmina had been so young and scared, but through it all she had been incredibly brave too, enough to give up her baby and build a new life all alone. Only a special person could overcome as much as Pashmina had. Sofie's eyes welled with pride.

"It was a mistake not to tell him herself," she agreed, somewhat soothing George's ruffled feathers, "but you were wrong too; sneaking off, leaving her and the baby alone like that."

George started to speak; he had heard enough about Pashmina and her troubles. It was time to say good-bye and go to work. *Baby, what baby?* He grabbed Sofie's arm. "Pashmina had a baby?"

Sofie stared at him as though she had seen a ghost, shocked and pale, and George felt her arm pull away from his grasp. "Oh shit, what have I done?" He watched her mumbling to no one in particular. "Shit, shit, shit!"

"Sofie?" He spoke gently, trying to calm them both. "What are you saying? Did Pashmina have a baby? Did she have my baby?"

Panicked, Sofie tried to recall what Pashmina had said about her run-in with George. She hadn't left anything out, describing how good he looked and what he'd been up to since she'd last seen him. She talked about the manuscript he left in her care, how good it was and how dangerous it would be if it ever became public, and then she'd told Sofie about Harry, and why he left. Because of George. They'd talked for a long time about that until Sofie's grandchildren came in from school. "I'm sorry, Pash, the kids just got home, and I've got to run." She blew a kiss into the phone and hung up before Pashmina could reply. Dammit! She'd just assumed Pashmina had told him about the baby.

Now he was waiting for her to answer him. No way, she'd said too much already. "Look, George, I have to go, but it was great seeing you." She turned on her heels, giving him a brilliant smile, and disappeared into the busy street, leaving George alone and gaping like a hooked fish.

* * *

George staggered backwards, nearly knocking into the Fish Stand. His mind was whirling as he tried to remember. Pashmina, Sofie, Harry…they all swirled together.

"Baby?" he thought. "What baby, whose baby?" The past rolled over him like a tsunami. Pashmina had never mentioned a baby.

After George left Greece, Pashmina had gone to the States to pursue her dream of becoming a writer, but that was all he knew. Had she remarried and had a family? She never said. And if that was the case, then why was she so upset with him? It didn't make sense.

Refocusing on the present, he headed back towards the *Cerilia* and Vasily who was standing impatiently by his boat, eager to get going. "George! We're waiting for you. Come on, let's go!"

George handed Vasily a pouch of chewing tobacco and grabbed the tether ropes. "I've got it, Vasily. Get on board."

Despite his girth, Vasily moved lightly onto the boat, yelling instructions to the crew for final preparations, and grabbing the ropes George threw his way. "Okay, George, climb aboard," he directed.

"I'm sorry, Vasily, I can't." The words escaped before George could stop them. The boat began to pull away. This was crazy. He was crazy. But he had to know: was he a father?

"George, what are you doing?" The sound of Vasily's voice snapped him back to attention. "Get on the boat!"

"There's something I have to do," George called, hating himself for letting Vasily down. "I'm sorry, but it's important and it can't wait."

Vasily looked disgusted but didn't argue. They'd been friends a long time. George was as dependable as the sun rising and setting every day. If he needed to attend to something, then Vasily wasn't going to stop him. He turned toward the bow of the boat. "Let's go," he said to the crew, "we've got work to do."

George left the docks and walked the short distance to his flat, a modest apartment, even by Greek standards, with a small living space and an even smaller bedroom; but after years of constant moving, it was home. He loved that his couch was comfortably worn from long-time use watching the flat screen t.v. across the room, reading, and napping. On the rare occasion he had friends over, a couple of mismatched chairs by the window paired with a reading table and lamp provided additional seating. Even the kitchen, equipped with the basic necessities and a two-person dining table, was cozy in his eyes.

Letting himself in, he walked purposefully to the bedroom and threw himself upon a full-sized bed covered by a lightweight, colorful quilt. A chest of drawers, the only other furniture in the room, stood nearby. He lay prone on the bed, one arm covering his eyes as if the pressure would help him to see.

"Pashmina," he whispered out loud, "what did you do?"

She had been so full of anger in the café, so fierce and dark. George had never seen her like that before. Definitely not how he had pictured their reunion. Unlike him, she seemed to have forgotten the sweetness of their past and couldn't be any less interested in a future together. But she really had cared about him once upon a time. She would have told him if there was a child, wouldn't she?

Pushing off the bed, he walked to the kitchen and grabbed a phone book from the counter. No doubt he could find what he needed at the Fish Stand, but at what price? It hadn't been easy keeping a low profile all these years, keeping even the most inquiring minds at bay. He couldn't risk calling attention to himself now. As long as he still had enemies, he wasn't taking any chances. Settling on a page, he ran a finger along the list of names, finally stopping at one.

"Dimitri Dicopolous. Private Investigator."

With shaky fingers, George dialed the number and waited for someone to answer.

"Hello. Dimitri Dicopolous' office, how may I help you?"

"I would like to speak to Mr. Dicopolous, please. I have a missing person I need to locate."

* * *

A sharp knock on the door broke the quiet of a lazy weekend morning. Several days had passed since George had contacted Dimitri Dicopolous' office and arranged to meet. Today was the day. Opening the door, he found a tall, thin man with white-tipped gray hair that stood on end, a Greek Don King. So much for a private investigator that blended in with the crowd.

"Mr. Levendakis?" Dimitri asked, extending a long arm.

"Yes. That's me." Extending his own calloused hand in greeting, George invited him in.

Dimitri entered the apartment and looked around, taking in every detail of his surroundings. It was a compact space, clean, neatly arranged, and efficient. Much like its resident, he suspected.

"Please, have a seat," said George, motioning to the chairs and table by the window. "Can I get you something to drink?" He placed a pitcher of ice water and two glasses in front of Dimitri and began to pour, his hand shaking slightly. These past few days had seemed endless waiting for this meeting. Now that it was finally happening, he was excited and scared at the same time.

"Thank you," said Dimitri, accepting the offered glass from George. He sipped slowly and watched as George fidgeted in the seat across from him. He smiled, understanding. "So you're probably thinking 'what happens now'?" George flushed, and Dimitri's smile grew broader. "Nothing to be embarrassed about, Mr. Levandakis. May I call you George? Absolutely nothing. People hire private investigators all the time for all manners of business. It's a specialty field, a skill, just like fishing or accounting. Now, how can I help you?"

"Well..." George stuttered. Where to begin? Despite his assurances, Dimitri was bound to think George was out of his freaking mind when he told the investigator of his quest. "I'm trying to locate a missing person, but I'm not sure if it's a male or a female. I don't have a name or a birth date, and I'm not entirely sure this person actually exists."

Dimitri looked closely at George. Was this a joke? "George, you know I'm a private investigator, not a magician, right?"

George kneaded his forehead and contemplated whether this was all a big mistake. Mistake or no, he needed to know if there had been a baby and if the baby was his. If there was any truth to the theory, he would worry about it after that.

"It's a long and complicated story, but I'll tell you all I know." A while later Dimitri stood up from his chair. George had told him everything he could and provided him with the most valuable piece of information: the name of Pashmina Papadakis.

"You understand this search must be conducted in the strictest confidence?" George underscored when they were finished. "I need to know if there was a child, but I'm not willing to destroy Pashmina's reputation to find out. It's so important that she never know that I'm looking."

"I'm a professional," Dimitri assured him. "No one will know that I even exist. I'll be in touch when I have something to share. In the meantime, call me if you think of anything else that might help my efforts."

* * *

Cleaning up after work one day, George heard the phone ring and stepped from the shower to answer it, wrapping a towel around his dripping body as he went. As he crossed the room, his stomach began to churn nervously. Was it the call he had been waiting for?

"Hello?"

"George? It's Dimitri. I've got some information for you but I don't think we should discuss it over the phone. Will you be home for a while?"

George's stomach knotted like a soft pretzel. He tried to imagine what Dimitri had discovered. "Yes, of course," he answered. "I'm in for the night. What time do you think you'll be here?"

"Give me 30 minutes," Dimitri answered. "I just have to finish up a few things here and I'll be right over."

Replacing the phone in its cradle, George sat roughly in a chair. He was numb. Dimitri sounded so urgent. Was it good news or bad and what did that even mean? Shocked at first to think he might be a father, he had recently started warming up to the idea, and now he had no idea how he would feel if there was no baby after all.

He picked up an old newspaper from the couch and quickly straightened the few pieces of furniture in the room before moving to the kitchen to clean up the unwashed dishes from breakfast. The fussing kept his mind busy and he relaxed a little, scrubbing and rinsing the dishes clean before placing them on the rack to dry.

A short time later he heard a knock on the door and went to open it for Dimitri who was waiting patiently on the other side, a manila folder in one hand. "Come in. Come in," George urged, ushering the investigator inside. "I've been going a little crazy since you called," he admitted, looking like a kid full of Christmas day anticipation.

Placing the folder on the table in front of him, Dimitri took a seat and smiled reassuringly at him. "I can't say this wasn't a challenging assignment, but that's what makes the job interesting, for me at least." Opening the folder, he began to sift through the papers inside until he found the one he was looking for. "Shall we get started?"

"Okay, George." Dimitri started in a professional tone, "First I ran a check on Pashmina and tried to track down what she's been doing for the last twenty-five years. The big picture you already know. She left Greece, immigrated to America, and eventually became an internationally known author. That part was easy. I have a file on her accomplishments and how her public life has been conducted. She's written a dozen books. The literary world loves her, and the public can't get enough of her."

"I knew she would make a great writer," George said softly. "She had the gift to write even as a young woman."

"And now everyone knows her talent." Dimitri passed George a piece of paper. "Here are all her published books and awards. She's lived most of her American life in Boston. Never married, or remarried, I should say. Okay, now to the real story. I checked further back, before her career took off, to see what I could find. I used Sofie's name and your name and Pashmina's family name to see if I could find any information."

"Which one of those names tipped you off?" George asked, curious to hear which angle opened the door to Dimitri's story.

"None of them," Dimitri answered.

George looked at him, confused. Someone's name had unlocked the door to the information in Dimitri's file.

"I found some information about Pashmina's early years. She moved to Boston in 1979 and lived in several city apartments over the next few years. She held two jobs prior to her writing career. She worked as an office clerk for the first few years, and then at a small publishing company. She did various jobs for them. If I had to guess, it was probably how she got her feet wet in the industry. By 1985, she had published her first novel. It was her third book "The Secret of the Volcano" that really got her noticed."

George folded his hands in his lap and nervously tapped his thumbs together. All of this information was interesting, but he probably could have found out most of it himself with the help of Google. He had hoped Pashmina would write her way to success. She had worked hard, and it seemed like that dream had been fulfilled.

"Now, here's where it gets interesting," Dimitri said, leaning towards George ever so slightly. "As I said, I had no real luck finding anything using your name or Pashmina's. But then when I was reviewing her file, I came across another name that I decided to try."

"What name?" George's mouth was so dry he could taste dust.

"Harry Lynch."

George furrowed his eyebrows and tapped his thumbs against each other even faster. Harry. Why would Harry's name trigger the secret door? Did that mean the baby Sofie spoke of was Harry's baby? Then why was she so upset? Was this search just a huge waste of time? And where was this mystery baby? Dimitri hadn't mentioned Pashmina having any children.

"What does Harry have to do with this?" George asked quietly.

"Well, I obviously discovered that Pashmina was married to Harry Lynch, so I decided to run a search on Harry. He and Pashmina divorced sometime in 1979. Harry married Catherine Spencer, a resident of London in 1980. They were married for 26 years until Harry passed away a few years ago from cancer. Harry and Catherine had two boys, Sean and Jonathan. They live in England, as does Catherine," Dimitri reported, as he looked over his notes.

"I still don't understand what Harry's name has to do with anything," George mumbled.

"Well, when I looked at 1979 birth records from Boston hospitals, I found Harry's name. There was a baby boy born on October 15, 1979 at Brigham & Women's hospital to a resident of Greece. The birth records were sealed. When I contacted the Massachusetts Open Adoption Registry, I found an application for exchanging information. The registry exists for adopted children to connect with birth parents." Dimitri took a deep breath, knowing that he was revealing a lot at once. George looked overwhelmed.

"So I applied to the registry for records pertaining to the baby boy born October 15th. It took a few days, but finally I received a copy of the birth certificate. It lists the mother as Pashmina Smith and the father as Harry Lynch."

"Pashmina Smith? Why Smith?" George asked.

"She was probably trying to keep her anonymity. It was Harry Lynch's name that caught my attention."

"What does that have to do with me?" George asked, the knot in his stomach slowly unfurling. Clearly, this search had revealed nothing that concerned him. Pashmina and Harry had a baby. So what?

"Well, I asked to have the records faxed to me. When they arrived, I discovered something very interesting," Dimitri countered.

"What?" George asked, already weary of the findings.

"When I received the actual birth certificate, Harry Lynch's name had been crossed out. The father listed on the birth certificate was you."

CHAPTER SIX

Amelia tapped the sheets of paper into a neat pile and placed them on the conference room table next to a tidy rainbow of pens and pencils. Satisfied her materials were in order, she turned her sights to the plump leather swivel chairs, and, for the fifth time in as many minutes, arranged them into strategic positions. She sipped on her Diet Coke and laughed nervously. "Relax," she chided herself, "it's just a conversation. You can do this."

Any minute now Pashmina would be here to review the manuscript, a standard part of the editorial process. Still, Amelia's nerves threatened to get the better of her, and she took another long and calming sip of soda. "I'm as ready as I'll ever be," she sighed heavily, glancing at her watch. "Let's get this show on the road."

"Good morning." Pashmina stood hesitantly in the doorway looking around the room. "May I come in, or am I interrupting? I heard voices."

Biting her lip to keep from laughing, Amelia greeted her, "Hi! Those weren't voices you heard, just me talking to myself. It helps me to think out loud sometimes," she explained.

"I know exactly what you mean." Understanding lit up Pashmina's face. "I often converse better with myself than other people."

Amelia motioned across the table for Pashmina to join her. "Please, have a seat. Can I get you something to drink before we start, coffee, tea, water?"

"I'm fine for the moment, thanks." Taking Amelia by surprise, Pashmina slipped into the chair beside her. "Do you mind if I sit next you?" she asked, laying a gentle hand on Amelia's arm. "It makes me feel like we're tackling this as a team."

"Fine by me." Pashmina's vulnerability was touching. One more reason Amelia was growing so fond of her.

"Good, then let's get to work. I'm sure you have a lot of questions for me." Taking another sip of soda, Amelia contemplated her next step. This was the moment she had been dreading, the moment she dared to challenge the Grand Dame herself. Amelia had been so excited to read the famous author's manuscript, feeling a little thrill each time she turned a page so crisp and smooth---she was editing Pashmina Papadakis' book!—she didn't even notice the difference, at first. But several pages in, after her initial excitement had tempered, and she was in full force editor mode, it was obvious. This new book wasn't like all the rest. It was dark, dangerous, and violent, a far cry from the lighthearted fun of a traditional Papadakis mystery.

Totally thrown, it took a while for Amelia to adjust to the new style, and even then she wasn't sure what to think. Sure, she liked it, but it was more than that, something was missing and that something was Pashmina. A random thought crossed her mind; did Pashmina really write it? She hated herself for even thinking something so improbable. But not impossible. Didn't Stuart say Pashmina had asked for an extension of her deadline? She'd been struck with severe writer's block. But then, at the last minute, she had delivered on schedule and Amelia, the most competent editor available, had earned the job.

Lucky her, or maybe not, since she now had the dubious task of figuring out if the manuscript was really Pashmina's. There was no way around it. Before they went any further, the question had to be asked.

Resigned, Amelia got right to the point. "Actually, I only have one question," she paused, "but it's a doozie."

Pashmina laughed. "Sounds ominous; go ahead, shoot."

"Well, the story is good, but not what I expected," Amelia said, choosing her words carefully. "It's so different from anything else you've done that I'm not quite sure what to make of it." Pashmina sat poised and calm. With a nervous laugh, Amelia summoned the courage to continue. "Is this manuscript even yours?"

Pashmina considered her answer carefully, silently batting it about like an inflated beach ball. Was the book hers? Yes, in every way but one. She had sacrificed everything for it, she had earned it. But she didn't write it; it was more like a gift, an opportunity to shed the pain and despair surrounding her since seeing George, again.

For months afterwards, Pashmina had been in a funk, reliving their fateful meeting over and over again, wondering how her life had gone so off course, and wishing desperately it had been different. But it wasn't. George had seen to that, betraying her as she had betrayed Harry; in the end neither one of them getting what they wanted. And then there was the baby, sweet and precious, the only innocent in the whole affair. If any good came out of this mess, it was the beautiful child lost to her.

Even now, it was hard to think about, and she blamed George for that as well, though the guilt and shame of her own actions haunted her too; mostly at night when her dreams took her places her waking mind dared not go. She imagined what the baby would look like now, no longer the tiny infant she had held for an instant, but an adult, fully grown. She imagined her child happy, the type of person who made others happy just by being around them, and good. Lord, let them be a good person she thought, a person of character, not like her and George.

But the evening bliss always dissipated at first light and in the morning she would wake up, tears dried and sticky on her face, her heart heavy in her chest. Pashmina knew she couldn't go on like this any longer. She had to restore balance to her life, put the past behind her, and though he didn't know it yet, George was going to help her do it. In a million years she would never forgive him for all that he had taken from her, but if her plan worked, she might manage to forget just a little and move on with her life.

The plan for her salvation had come to her in a dream, swift and sudden, telling her exactly what to do. It was simple really. She would publish George's manuscript as her own, thereby fulfilling her commitment to Dewes and let fate take it from there. If it caused trouble for George, tough; payback's a bitch. She would consider it his way of making up for all the pain and upset he had caused.

Pashmina met Amelia's inquisitive gaze, and wondered how long she had been waiting for her to answer. The girl was fidgeting slightly in her seat, growing anxious, and Pashmina felt bad for keeping her waiting. She liked Amelia very much and was growing fonder of her by the day. Amelia was kind, and clearly concerned that Pashmina might be stepping into harm's way. Gentle in demeanor but strong too, she had the courage to ask the tough questions, and was astute enough to know which ones to ask. But not quite all of them.

"Yes, the book is mine," Pashmina said at last. "I know it's a different style for me, but think of it as an experiment. I take full responsibility for *Family Secrets*.

Her conviction was contagious, melting away Amelia's nervous tension. "I believe you and I trust you," she said simply. "Now, let's get started.

CHAPTER SEVEN

Chadwick Brown strode confidently through the hallways of Brown Books, surveying his domain like a proud king measuring his realm. In the few years since he and Abby had inherited the reins of power from their father, they had wasted no time flexing their youthful muscles to flip the ultra-conservative firm on its head. Under their direction, more aggressive operating procedures were now in place, as well as an exciting new roster of fresh and contemporary authors who gave the company a unique progressive edge.

He glanced around approvingly. Yes, they were doing well, but the competition was never far behind, and heavy-handed pressure from the Board, i.e. his Chairman father, never stopped. Chad had the ulcers to prove it.

Behind a massive desk, his secretary Lauren sat like a sentry guarding the inner sanctum that was his office. She looked up as he approached, a pile of pink message slips in one hand, a steaming cup of coffee in the other. "Good morning, Mr. Brown," she smiled, handing him both items at once. "Your father called. He'd like to speak with you about the agenda for the upcoming Board of Directors meeting." Chad grimaced and sighed, "Anything else?"

With a sympathetic smile Lauren deftly changed the subject of his father to something far more dangerous. "Careful drinking your coffee," she warned. "It's very hot. I almost melted my tongue on mine. Oh, and your 9:30 appointment, Mr. Smith, is waiting in your office."

Damn. He had totally forgotten Tim was coming in today. "Thanks," Chad said, glancing at the message from his father. This conversation with Tim would have to be short. Chad didn't have time to think about someone else's problems, he had enough of his own. "Do me a favor?" he asked Lauren. "Buzz me in half an hour and say I have another meeting or something Okay?" Flashing his brightest smile, Chad headed to his office.

*   *   *

Surveying the city skyline from the 360-vantage of Chad's 20th story office, Tim felt powerful, invincible, and he liked it. This was where he belonged, at the top calling the shots. After all, there's no 'I' in team but there is in 'Tim.' He chuckled softly at his own joke, turning as the door opened and Chad entered the room.

Chad looked older than Tim remembered. He noted the distinguished gray already dusting Chadwick's temples and the crow's feet fanning from the corners of his colorless eyes; eyes that could appear as clear as a mountain spring on a sunny day or as dark as a raging sea depending upon his mood. Right now they were neither light nor dark just a little cloudy and distant, as though his mind was elsewhere. He was impeccably dressed as always in a pewter gray pin-striped suit custom-fit to his long lean frame with a silver gray shirt and black silk tie. He reminded Tim of a Navy destroyer: strong, bold, menacing.

"Hey, Tim, how long's it been?" Chad asked, hastily shaking Tim's hand and guiding him to a chair in front of his desk.

"I've been trying to figure that out myself," Tim replied, giving his best impression of a friendly smile, and ignoring Chad's obvious efforts to hasten things along. "I guess that means too long."

"Well, you look good." He gave Tim a cursory once-over. "Not a single gray hair in that obstinate head of yours." Self-consciously Chad smoothed a hand across his own silver strands. "Hard work and stress, they'll get you every time," he explained.

Tim bristled. Chad was in rare form, lobbing insults like tennis balls before they'd barely said 'hello'. "Not to mention the painful trappings of legacy," Tim countered, looking pointedly around the lavishly handsome office. "Must be Hell."

Chad scowled, so briefly Tim thought he might have imagined it, until he met the other man's granite stare. Shifting uncomfortably in the chair Tim cursed his stupidity; this was no time for a pissing match with Chad, not when he needed his help. "Sorry," he apologized ruefully, hands raised in surrender. "Bad joke."

Chad lowered his gaze and sifted through the stack of phone messages still clasped in his hand as Tim squirmed in front him like a kid who had to pee. He smirked. Let him twist in the wind for a bit. He deserved it. Sure, Chadwick Brown IV enjoyed a life of privilege and entitlement, but no one could accuse him of being a slacker, least of all Tim Smith.

'Buddy' wasn't a word he would use synonymously with Tim. They weren't close in the traditional sense. Tim never let anyone get too close, and he wasn't a trusted confidante like Ben, but at one time, he'd been a savior when Chad needed saving the most. A debt Chad would never be able to repay.

On a Sunday morning during their senior year, he and Tim were alone in the apartment; Ben was on a road trip to New York City. Desperately seeking coffee, Chad had stumbled to the kitchen where Tim was already on the job of making brew. Wordlessly he handed Chad a steaming mug, turning back to pour one for himself. Without Ben's unifying presence, they were silent but civil.

When Chad's cell phone rang, Tim headed to his room, only too happy to escape the chatter of Chad's weekly conversations with his mom.

Every Sunday she called him, and every Sunday Tim tried to ignore the envy churning inside him. Chad had it all: money, power, and a mother who loved him.

"You're lying!" Chad's scream curdled down the hall to Tim's room. "Why are you saying this? You're lying!" Tiptoeing to the kitchen, Tim felt like an eavesdropper. He had heard Chad angry before, usually with his dad, but this was different, almost like a primal wailing. Tim rounded the corner and almost tripped over Chad, who was sitting hunched on the floor, his head and torso folded over his knees. He was sobbing.

Squatting next to him, Tim put a hand on Chad's shoulder. "Hey, what's going on?" Chad's heart was pounding beneath Tim's hand and his own seized with dread. "Chad, buddy, what's up? Talk to me."

Chad's face was barely recognizable, ravaged by the tears streaming down it. He struggled to speak. "My mom," his voice broke. "My mom is dead, car crash. How can that be?" He had to be dreaming. In a minute he would wake up and everything would be normal again. He watched Tim pick up the phone he had dropped moments before.

"Okay, I understand. I'll take care of him, Mr. Brown, and I'm very sorry for your loss, sir." Tim shut the phone and looked somberly at Chad. This wasn't a nightmare; it was real.

Coming to terms with Chad's new reality took a long time, and a lot of therapy. Through it all, Tim was there; listening when Chad needed to talk, comforting when no one else knew what to say, and giving him space when he was suffocated by concerned friends. For those first few months after his mother's death, Tim was his anchor, and Chad felt closer to him than anyone, even Abby. Always daddy's little girl, his twin sister seemed to be doing fine.

In time, things returned to somewhat normal. Chad mastered keeping his grief to himself by focusing on his studies, and enjoying the dwindling days of freedom before his life sentence at Brown Books began. Once he had tried to share his deepest fear with Tim: what if Chad wasn't good enough, what if he couldn't do it? But Tim had moved on, too, taking his understanding and compassion with him.

"You know, a lot of people would kill to be in your shoes, to have a dad who gives half a shit as much as yours." Chad was stunned. What happened to the guy with the sixth sense for knowing what to say, what to do to get him through his despair? Something shifted and instantly they were back to their old arm's length relationship.

"So what's up?" Chad asked. He leaned comfortably back in his chair and looked at Tim, wincing as he tried to sip the still-scalding coffee.

"I'm looking for an opportunity," Tim replied, staring longingly at Chad's steaming cup. Just as well he hadn't been offered anything to drink. He was nervous enough without any additional caffeine jitters. "I'm ready to take another step on the career path, maybe even change direction altogether. Ben thought I should speak with you about it," he added.

Thanks Ben. "Is that so?" Chad asked, brushing his annoyance aside.

"And I think Ben's right. You and I do have something to talk about."

"You mean a job? Here at Brown?"

"I mean a career. A career that gives me everything I want by helping you get what you need. I have what it takes, Chad," Tim said eagerly, leaning forward in his chair, "the knowledge, the experience and, frankly, the balls to do what it takes to keep Brown Books at the top of the publishing pyramid. I assume that's what you want, or rather, isn't that what you have to do?"

Chad closed his eyes and opened them again. For an instant, it sounded like Chadwick III was talking to him. His father never missed an opportunity to remind him of his responsibilities to the company, to the family. He didn't need Tim prodding him too.

Tim watched Chad closely, fairly certain his words had found their mark; despite Chad's best efforts to liberate himself, duty to family would always come first. Burdened by birthright and the expectations that went along with it, and handicapped by insecurities, Chad was an afflicted man; he knew it and Tim knew it.

"When did you become an authority on publishing?" Chad asked. "Last I knew you were in advertising."

"I am. But I've become something of an expert thanks to one of my clients, Dewes Publishing. Ever heard of them?" he teased. Chad frowned, but motioned for him to continue. "For the past two years I've been the senior executive on that account."

"Their advertising's pretty good," Chad conceded.

"Good? It's outstanding! My campaigns have won awards, they've transformed authors into rock stars, they've turned dusty classics into must-have titles. Most importantly," Tim paused dramatically, "they've made new releases fly better than a witch on a broomstick."

"Okay, I got it," Chad assured him. "Obviously you've got some idea of what you're doing, but there's a lot more to this business than just advertising, you know."

"That's true, but to create really effective advertising like mine you have to know everything about your product: the good, the bad, and the ugly. Since I took charge of the Dewes account, I've made a point of learning the ins and outs of their business, what they do, how they do it and why." Tim paused. Did he sound too intense, too desperate? Forcing himself to relax, he joked, "I'm so committed to serving my client 24/7, I'm even dating one of their editors."

Chad smiled tightly as he listened to Tim's pitch. It didn't take a genius to figure out that Tim was loyal to no one but himself, but Chad was beginning to understand why Ben had sent him here. Tim was sharp and he was shrewd. But could Chad depend on him?

"Sounds like you've got a real inside track at Dewes, why don't you just go there?"

"One word," said Tim. "Amelia. Right now she's my girlfriend, but if I worked at Dewes too, it could get awkward."

"For sure." Chad nodded over tented fingers. Maybe he could repay an old debt after all and make it work to his benefit.

"Mr. Brown, you have another meeting in five minutes," Lauren interrupted through the intercom.

The two men looked at each other, their veiled expressions revealing nothing of one's growing excitement and the other's growing interest. "Thank you, Lauren," Chad answered smoothly. "Would you please reschedule? Mr. Smith and I have some more business to discuss."

"And how about some coffee?" Tim added, relaxing for the first time since the conversation began.

Chad nodded, "And more coffee please, Lauren." They were going to need it.

CHAPTER EIGHT

George folded the last of his shirts, neatly placing it on top of his open suitcase. He had packed clothes for a week, all the time he could afford, hoping it was enough to find his son. He added a small toiletry bag filled with soap and shaving provisions and zippered the old canvas piece of luggage shut. Once inseparable, he hadn't so much as looked at the case in years, but they were reunited now for what could be the most important trip of his life.

He pulled the shades over the apartment windows, checking that everything was in order, then picked up the suitcase and headed for the front door and the taxi waiting outside. As he slid into the backseat, he did a quick inventory: passport, check; ticket, check; dossier with notes and findings from Dimitri's investigation, check.

Dimitri had been very thorough and organized, giving George last minute instructions and trying to help as much as he could. "It's not going to be easy, but start your search with the Massachusetts Open Adoption Agency. If they can't help you, try the Department of Motor Vehicles and the hospital where the baby was born," he had directed. "One of them must have something that can help you find your son."

So much to do and so little time, but if George found what he was looking for, it would all be worth it in the end.

* * *

George exited The Hotel Stratford, a modest little place recommended by the Airport Visitors Center, and for now, his temporary home. Nestled among the tree-lined streets of the South End, it was clean, affordable, and centrally located, an easy walk to all the places he needed to go. First stop, the Massachusetts Open Adoption Agency.

The Agency was housed in a large brick building several decades old. The façade was ornate but tired looking, its white paint flaking and peeling in places. George double checked the address to make sure he had the right place.

Inside, he scanned the faded and worn lobby directory, and made his way to the third floor. Suite 302 was bathed in fluorescent light that flooded the darkest corners of the small waiting room, revealing several worn chairs and a few tables littered with dog-eared magazines. He looked around and spotted a registration desk with a sign instructing him to 'Please Check in Here.' Hesitantly, George approached and waited for the large woman sitting behind the glass partition to notice him.

"May I help you?" she asked, adjusting a pair of tortoise shell glasses that had slipped to the end of her nose.

"I'm here to see Merrilee Swanson," he replied, slightly intimidated.

"Do you have an appointment?"

Cursing silently, he fumbled through his pockets for the paper with the Agency's information on it. Stupid, stupid, it hadn't even occurred to him to make an appointment. "No, I'm sorry, I didn't know I needed one. But please," he implored, "I have talk to Ms. Swanson, it's important. I've come all the way from Greece to find my son and I need her help. Please."

Unmoved, the receptionist shifted forward for a closer look at him. Emotions of steel were the number one requirement of this job which had brought her face-to-face with heart-wrenching sob stories every day for more than a decade. She had seen and heard just about everything, every excuse, every lie, every desperate plea for help, and to her trained eye, Mr. Handsome's anxious despair was the real deal. She gestured for George to take one of the chairs that lined the wall.

"Have a seat. I'll see if Merrilee's available." With a sigh of relief George plopped into one of the empty chairs to wait, and focused on keeping his nerves at bay. Ms. Swanson just had to help him.

What seemed like an eternity later, the receptionist lumbered back down the hallway towards him. Reclaiming her chair, she adjusted her glasses and motioned for George to come back to the glass partition.

"You're a very lucky man, Mr...," she paused waiting for him to fill in the blank.

"Levendakis. George Levendakis."

"Mr. Levendakis," she repeated. "Merrilee's just finishing up some paperwork and then she'll see you. You can take a seat until she's free."

He sat down again fidgeting impatiently. So much depended on the outcome of this meeting and the clock was ticking. If they didn't have the information he needed, he would have to move on and quickly. Now that he was here, the idea of heading home without finding his son was unthinkable.

A door by the reception desk opened slowly and a female head poked around it. "Mr. Levendakis?" the woman asked.

"Yes." George jumped to his feet.

Petite with a long blond braid accessorizing her shoulder like an epaulet, she emerged from behind the door neatly dressed in black pants and a blue blouse, a stack of folders tucked under her arm.

"I'm Merrilee," she said, extending her hand, and invited George to follow her down the hallway. "My office is this door on the right. Let's go in and have a seat."

She waited until George was settled in another drab office chair before taking her own seat behind the desk. She smiled. "What can I do for you, Mr. Levendakis? I don't usually see people without an appointment, but Sharon mentioned you're here from Greece and that's rather unusual for this office."

"I'm here to find my son." Nervous, George decided to get right to the point.

"What makes you think he's missing?"

"He's not missing." George replied. "I just don't know where he is or who he is for that matter. I'm hoping you can help me find him." He knew it sounded lame but continued anyway. "I have reason to believe he was born here in Boston in 1979. His mother and I were involved, but we broke up before then and she never told me about the baby."

Taking notes, Merrilee found her growing curiosity spawned a host of fresh questions. "How do you know she gave birth? Why do you think you're the father? How do you think I can help you?"

He opened his hand to reveal a paper deeply creased from repeated reading and refolding. "Because I'm listed on his birth certificate," he said, handing it to her.

"How did you get this?" Merrilee asked, examining it for legitimacy.

"I hired a private investigator. He found this birth certificate from 1979 certifying that a boy was born at Brigham and Women's Hospital in October and listing me as his father. The mother on the certificate is the woman I was in a relationship with, but as I said, she never told me anything."

"The investigator also learned that someone had registered with your agency to exchange information. I assume it was Pashmina trying to find our child too. What I need to know is if you have any information you can share with me?"

Merrilee studied him carefully. Clearly this wasn't a joke, and judging from his expression, he was seriously determined to find his son. "Okay, George," she said at last, "I need your personal identification and any other relevant information you have on this. I'll run it through the computer and see what we can find out."

For the first time in weeks he felt relieved. He had a partner now, someone to share the burden, someone who could help. "Thank you," he choked.

Helping people like George was one of the few perks of Merrilee's job. Swallowing the lump in her throat, she said, "I'm going to need a little time to work on this. Why don't you go take a walk, grab some lunch, and meet me back here at 12:30?"

George grabbed her hand tightly. "Thank you, Ms. Swanson. I'm so grateful, more than you'll ever know."

Merrilee watched him go. He had a bounce in his step she hadn't noticed earlier. It was up to her now to keep it there. No pressure. She sat down again facing her computer. "Okay," she whispered, "let's see what we can find."

* * *

George stepped outside, breathing deeply, filling his lungs with Beantown air. Since running into Sofie, George felt like he had been holding his breath, waiting to learn the truth, but he felt better now thanks to Dimitri and Merrilee. Glancing at his watch, and mindful of the time, he began to walk, not caring which way he went as long as it was forward.

The streets of Boston were a nice change of pace from the docks and decks that shaped his world at home, and George was eager to explore the city where his son was born and Pashmina had settled. It was easy to see its appeal. On a trolley tour he discovered the diversity of its neighborhoods like the quaint Beacon Hill, the historic North End, and the homey familiarity of the Seaport District. City life wasn't for him anymore, but it was certainly a nice place to visit.

The food here wasn't too shabby either with countless restaurants, cafes, delis and bakeries, each one looking more delicious than the one he had just passed. But it was getting late, and he was hungry, so in the interest of time he ducked into a small sandwich shop to grab some lunch. He ate at a counter lined with stools and a large window looking out on a busy street filled with cars and people walking alone, in pairs, and even groups, all in a hurry to get somewhere.

What about Pashmina? Was she somewhere out there, too? Not for the first time he wondered what she would do if she saw him here. Not be too happy was probably an understatement, judging from their last encounter but he didn't give a shit. Not anymore. Not since he found out she had deliberately kept him in the dark all these years.

He glanced at his watch. Time to get back to Merrilee and her magical computer. Excitement began to build inside him as he tossed his sandwich wrapper in the trash and headed back to the agency.

A short time later, he let himself back into Suite 302, surprised to see the waiting room bustling with people talking quietly or zoning out, lost in their own private worlds. He marched confidently this time up to the registration desk and asked to see Merrilee, who called to him from her office. "Come on back, George."

Nervous again, he made his way into her office hoping for the best but bracing for the worst. Merrilee looked up at him and smiled. "Well, George," she said, pulling papers from various piles on her desk, "I have some good news for you. I have the name of your son."

He had imagined this moment so many times but still it caught him off guard. Tears spilled down his cheeks and his heart lifted like a helium balloon.

"George? Are you okay?" Merrilee asked, pulling a box of tissues from her desk.

Okay? George laughed out loud, sounding a little hysterical, happy hysterical. "Never better. I have a son!"

"You do indeed," she affirmed, "and his name is Timothy Smith." She let it sink in before continuing. "In 1979, private adoptions or children who were wards of the State typically had sealed birth certificates that were closed and inaccessible to everyone. So even if you'd been looking for your son when he was little, it would have been almost impossible for you to find him. Fortunately, times have changed and although technically these records are still sealed, when someone registers with us, they can provide us with whatever personal information they want."

"When I checked the birth date you gave me against the hospital's records, I found that someone had registered new information into our Open Adoption Records data bank." George stared at her blankly, and she hurried to explain. "The data bank holds names, dates, and places that birth parents or adoptees can provide in case someone is looking for them. In your case, Timothy Smith's name and birth date were entered into the system ten years ago. It appears no one has tried to access the information before today, but someone's been hoping to put the pieces of the puzzle together for a long time."

George paused for a moment. "Pashmina? She must have looked for him. Does it say if she ever found Timothy?"

"No, George," Merrilee answered quietly, sensing his disappointment. "No one by the name of Pashmina has ever contacted our organization. The data bank information was left by Timothy Smith."

For the second time that day George's emotions did a free-fall. He didn't know this Pashmina who kept secrets, who gave up their child and never looked back. Poker-faced he looked down at the paper Merrilee had given him.

"That's the information your son left with the Agency," she pointed out. "As you can see, it's his name and an update with what looks like a work address. Makes sense if you want to be found but aren't sure what kind of a person might be looking for you. Can't be too careful with family, you know," she joked feebly as George continued to stare at the paper. She tried again to boost his spirits. "Look, George, I know it's not a lot to work with. Timothy may not even work at this address anymore, but you have his name and that's a great place to start."

The cloud covering George's face made way for his bright smile. "Merrilee, honestly, I can't thank you enough for all you've done for me today; I promise I won't let your hard work go to waste. I will find Timothy."

Merrilee stood and shook his hand. "That's thanks enough for me; I'm just happy for you. Now go find your son."

CHAPTER NINE

Returning to his office, Tim barely noticed the lone figure sitting in Trillingham's reception area. He was still thinking about the meeting he had just left. The last of his account wrap-ups, these 'good-bye' meetings were protocol when an account manager moved on, and he had been having a good time with it, feeling like weights were being lifted as he geared up for his big move to Brown Books. But this last one had been hard.

From Tim's earliest days on the Dewes account, Stuart Gould had taken Tim under his wing, mentoring and teaching him all about the publishing industry. How did Tim return the favor? By taking everything he had learned about marketing for publishing and putting it to work for the competition. He knew some people would see it as a harsh move, and Tim had been nervous about breaking the news to Stuart. But he shouldn't have worried. Stuart was his usual classy self, making Tim feel guilty and relieved when he said, "Brown's lucky to have you, Tim. I know you'll do great things for them."

It was the kind of thing a father would say, and Tim's chest puffed slightly at the thought. "Tim," the receptionist called him over. "There's a man waiting to see you. He doesn't have an appointment and wouldn't let me schedule one. He says it's important." Shrugging, she pointed towards the waiting area.

Tim turned to look at the only other person in the room, a man neatly dressed in khakis and a plaid button down shirt. Casually flipping through the pages of a magazine, he seemed relaxed despite his left leg bouncing up and down like a jack hammer. It was hard to get a good look at the man's downturned face, but he didn't look familiar. "What's his name?" Tim asked the receptionist.

"Levendakis. Do you know him?"

Tim shook his head, "I don't think so, but I guess I'll find out." He walked over to the magazine-reading, leg-tapping man. "Mr. Levendakis?"

Hearing his name, George's head snapped back so he was face-to-face with Timothy Smith. He stared hard, not wanting to look away from his son. His son! Who was looking back at him, curious but guarded, with his mother's beautiful brown eyes. Grabbing Tim's extended hand like a lifeline, George moved in for a closer look. The dark, wavy hair, the muscular build, the confident set of his shoulders; it was him twenty years ago. Almost. Unlike him, this young man emanated a cool reserve that warned 'don't get too close,' instantly squelching George's impulse to wrap him in a fierce bear hug.

"Yes, that's me. And you're Timothy Smith?" Obviously.

"Call me Tim," he said, creating a little space between them. Levendakis was staring at him like a big, juicy steak. "How can I help you?"

"I'd like to talk to you if you have a minute," George answered, looking skeptically around the lobby. "Somewhere a little more private maybe?"

A small frown formed between Tim's eyes as he considered George's request. The look reminded George of Pashmina weighing her options before making a decision.

"Sure," Tim offered at last. "We can talk in my office. This way." He turned, leaving George to follow, his heart pounding, mind racing. All the times George had imagined this moment, he had never gotten past this point. What did he do now?

In Tim's office, he offered George a seat then sat himself, keeping the large, wooden desk between them. "So," Tim started, "are you looking for an advertising agency, Mr. Levendakis?"

"Not exactly." George's palms were damp with sweat, his mouth dry as a bone. "I've actually been looking for you."

Keeping his face carefully blank, Tim studied the man more intently. Who was this guy? He shook his head confused, "I'm sorry, I don't understand."

Just three little words and both their lives would be changed forever. George was tongue-tied. And terrified. Hiding from his past seemed like a piece of cake compared to confronting his future. Did he really want this? Could he handle being a father now, after all this time? Most guys had a chance to grow with their kids, but Tim was no kid. He was an adult, a grown man and George knew absolutely nothing about him.

Walk away. That's what George should do before he screwed everything up. Like hell. He had come too far to leave now. "There's no delicate way to say this, so I'm just going to say it: Tim, I'm your father."

There it was. With a sigh of relief, George glanced anxiously at his son, still expressionless and silent. He seemed to be taking it well. Or maybe not. A burst of hysterical laughter suddenly filled the room.

"Good one," Tim applauded. "So, where's the camera?" Still laughing, he searched his desk, looking inside his coffee mug and under the calendar blotter. Giving up, he looked at George. "And what talent agency are you from? I'll admit, there's a good resemblance. Thanks for giving me an idea of what I'll look like in another twenty years or so."

Bemused, George could barely answer. "I don't know what you're talking about."

"My farewell video, you know, good-bye, good luck in the new job. That's what this is, right?" Thank God, because Tim was starting to get a little creeped out by this guy.

Listening to Tim, George understood. His son was leaving the agency. Well, thank God George had found him first. "Congratulations on your new job." He smiled, "but I'm not here for a video and, I'm not an actor from a talent agency. I'm your biological father."

The shock was obvious. Tim looked stunned, and George kept talking to give him time to catch his breath, "I just found out too," George explained. "How, it doesn't really matter, but as soon as I knew, I did everything I could to find you. And now here we are." He smiled anxiously, searching his son's face for signs of life, wondering if he had heard a word he said.

Tim's head was about to burst with everything that was happening. He had hoped and prayed for this, or something like it, but never believed it would really happen. Didn't they always say be careful what you wish for? "What makes you think I don't have a father?" he questioned, taking stock of George with fresh eyes. George looked honest and sincere.

George stood. Removing a folded paper from his back pocket, he smoothed it open with shaking hands and handed it to Tim. "This is your birth certificate. As you can see, I'm listed as your birth father."

It looked official enough with the insignia of the Commonwealth of Massachusetts. Tim could see that he was born at Brigham and Women's Hospital and the date of birth was the same as the one he celebrated every year. "Where did you get this?" Tim asked, his voice a strained whisper.

George's heart went out to him. He knew all too well what it was like to have your world turned upside down without warning. Another thought struck him. What about Tim's family? Did he know he was adopted, or had George just delivered the one-two punch himself with the birth certificate?

What they needed was time to sort through this together. "It's a long and pretty incredible story," George said, answering Tim's question carefully. "Have dinner with me, and I'll tell you everything I know."

*   *   *

George and Tim waited as the waitress placed their drinks in front of them, ice water for George, vodka on the rocks for Tim. George thanked her, sending her away before he changed his mind and switched to something harder. What he needed was a clear head. This dinner was too important to mix with alcohol.

Clearing his throat, George hesitated, "I'm not sure where to start."

Neither was Tim. The cab ride there had been bad enough, awkward silence occasionally punctuated by his best tour guide voice politely pointing out sites of interest. At the restaurant, they had settled comfortably into this booth and begun a lengthy discussion of the menu before chatting up the waitress with their drink and dinner orders. As if it was the most important thing in the world, as if they had nothing else to talk about. Truth was Tim was afraid; he suspected they both were.

"Maybe you should start at the beginning," Tim suggested, "and we'll see how it goes from there."

George agreed. "Well, I guess this story starts at the end. As I've said, I live in Greece in a village called Cronilys. I'm a fisherman now, but I wasn't always. Anyway, a few weeks ago, I was in the market and ran into an old acquaintance, Sofie, a dear friend of your mother's actually. We hadn't seen each other in years, and we got to talking about your mother and things that'd happened between us. The conversation got heated."

He paused. "I loved your mother very much, but she could be stubborn. Sofie told me I was selfish for leaving her alone and pregnant." He still couldn't believe it. Shaking his head he continued, "I didn't know what

Sofie was talking about, and she ran away before I could ask her. I went nuts thinking about it."

"My first thought was to contact your mother, but we're not exactly on speaking terms," he said dryly. "And the last time I saw her she didn't say anything about a baby. So I hired a private investigator instead. I wanted to know if there really was a baby and if it was mine." He took a sip of water and braced himself for the finish. "I finally heard from him a few days ago. He'd found your birth certificate naming me as the father."

The frown was back, nestled between Tim's eyes. "What happened between you and my mother? Why did you leave her?"

The waitress served their meals, efficiently placing plates of steak frites in front of each of them, which gave George a moment to collect his thoughts. "In a nutshell, my life was in danger, and I had to get out of Greece immediately. Otherwise, I promise you, I'd never have left her."

"But you're not together now?" Tim sipped his drink, not the least bit interested in eating.

George sighed. This was even harder than he thought. "No, we're not. She wanted to be with her husband."

Choking, Tim's throat burned with vodka and his eyes watered. "Excuse me?"

His cheeks flaming red, George squirmed in his seat. They were both adults, but he felt like a kid caught with his pants down. "Your mother and I weren't married."

"No shit." Tim's voice dripped sarcasm. "Then how do you know you're the father and not.....?"

"Harry Lynch was her husband, and he's not the father," George said, wincing at Tim's caustic words. "*I'm* your father. I know this because it says so on the birth certificate, and because I feel it in my gut."

Tim played with his food, pondering the facts that were starting to chip away at his wall of doubt. But there was more to the story. "Even if the birth certificate's legit, that doesn't explain how you found me."

"The Massachusetts Open Adoption Agency," George reminded him gently. "You registered there a few years ago. They told me your name and where you work."

Tim had registered with the agency like a million years ago, or at least it felt that way, occasionally updating the information just in case and hoping something like this would come of it, hoping his parents would find him. He chewed slowly on a piece of steak. "Okay, so who's my mother?"

Tim's expression was hopeful, he was starting to believe, and it made George sad. Of course Tim wanted to know about his mother, but what could George tell him? He didn't know why she had given her baby up and he didn't know why she hadn't tried to find him since. Pashmina's story wasn't his to tell.

"Your mother was an incredible woman, young and beautiful when I met her. I was a reporter at the time, speaking on a panel about writing professionally. I spotted her in the audience, and I couldn't take my eyes off her."

A small smile touched his face as George remembered. "Afterwards we spoke, and the connection was immediate. We started working together, me as her writing coach and teacher, she as my muse, my inspiration. You see, she wanted to become a novelist and I was trying to branch out with my writing as well."

"Your mother was married by this point, but her husband was a naval officer. He'd been away for several months already when we met and she was lonely; writing was her escape." He looked tentatively at Tim paying rapt attention, not eating or drinking. "I guess I probably took advantage of the situation, but I fell in love with her hard and fast, and for a while I thought she loved me too. I didn't want to believe her when she said she loved her husband and we were quote unquote 'over'."

"So then what, what did you do?" Tim had to remind himself these were his parents they were talking about and not a sappy soap opera.

"And then I disappeared." Tim looked dumbfounded and George laughed.

"I thought it would be temporary, that I'd be home soon and I'd win her back, but I was wrong. I didn't see her again for more than twenty years."

They were straying off topic but Tim's curiosity was piqued. "Why did you have to disappear?"

George ate his steak, stalling for time while he weighed his options. Telling Tim the truth was risky, especially since things seemed to be going pretty well between them. They were getting to know each other; in time maybe Tim would even trust him. But right now the truth could be devastating to their fragile relationship.

He waived the waitress over. He had come this far, too late to turn back. "This could take a while. I need a drink."

CHAPTER TEN

Beads of sweat were beginning to form on George's forehead. It was late morning and the temperature was already soaring past eighty degrees, but he wasn't sure if it was the heat or his nerves getting to him. Leaning against his car, an old 1972 Ford Mercury, he was a few minutes early for his meeting Christoff. One thing George knew for certain, punctuality was key in this line of work, a matter of life or death even. Only a fool would test Christoff's limits on this, and George was no fool. In fact, despite his harsh tone and threatening demeanor, George sensed Christoff was softening towards him. That was a good thing because the sooner he earned Christoff's trust, the sooner he would be able to end this crazy escapade.

Five weeks earlier George had volunteered to infiltrate and uncover the inner workings of one of the most notorious organized crime families in Greece, the Adelphos. By far the most powerful and brutal organization of its kind, the Adelphos was also the most enigmatic of all the groups. With its members sworn to an impregnable vow of silence, and an under-the-radar operations strategy, the tight-lipped, stealthy Adelphos was becoming something of interest to more than a few. George had decided this would be his mission, the story that would catapult his career as a journalist and a writer. Despite the danger.

Just getting his foot in the door had taken some time, calling in favors and debts to get the operation started. Finally, a lead on a small time gangster had connected him with Christoff, a twenty-something 'made man' who owed his life to the organization. Thinking George was a second cousin of a deceased member of the Adelphos, Christoff had grudgingly agreed to 'sponsor' George, wasting no time inducting him into a treacherous world of drug deals and shakedowns.

But that was just the tip of the iceberg. George knew Christoff was testing him, deciding whether or not the newcomer could be trusted, and he had been doing his best to prove himself. Now it seemed maybe he had. Christoff's last message was cryptic but promising.

Suddenly a car pulled up alongside him, and the driver rolled down his window. It was Christoff. "Get in, quickly!" he instructed as George climbed rapidly into the passenger seat beside him. He looked at Christoff, who drove, jaw clenched.

"Is everything all right?" George asked nervously.

"We have work to do. Now listen carefully. Do exactly what I tell you and you'll be fine. Screw it up and it'll be your ass on the line; you'll be answering to the Adelphos. Understand?"

Perfectly. What they were about to do was dangerous and undoubtedly illegal, and George was flying solo, risking everything for this assignment. If things went south, no one would help him, not even the newspaper, though his editor had promised to contact the police in the case of an emergency. Wonderful. He felt safe now.

The car screeched away from the curb and headed into the town of Piraeus. Christoff said very little as they navigated the narrow streets, passing through a large marketplace where stalls were lined up displaying fruits and vegetables. Vendors were calling out loudly to people, enticing them to come closer and buy their produce. Christoff slowed the car, staring intently at the people on the sidewalk. At the last stall, he pulled the car over quickly, almost hitting an older woman who was gathering bags around her.

George grabbed the edge of his seat as the car came to a sudden stop and a young man hopped into the back of the car. He wore a cap over his eyes and sported the beginnings of a stubbly beard.

Nodding towards George with a voice that rumbled like thunder, he asked, "Is this the guy?"

George extended his hand, but was stopped short by a pair of beady eyes glaring back at him. He blinked. Did that booming bass really belong to this little shrew of a man?

"Yes." Christoff answered gruffly as he pulled away from the curb again. No one spoke further and the prolonged silence made George uneasy. He had no idea where they were going but he sure as hell wasn't going to ask either of these guys. The car headed toward the center of Piraeus, the streets growing gradually wider as they approached the center of town. They passed several large buildings that George knew well: the main post office, a few banks, and finally, a large stone building that was home to several law firms. Christoff pulled around the corner and parked.

"Stay here," he commanded, exiting the driver's seat and slamming the door behind him. The other guy or 'The Shrew' as George decided to call him, followed suit as Christoff rapped his knuckles on George's window, signaling him to open it.

"We're going in this building for a minute. I want you to get behind the wheel and wait for us to come out. When we do, you drive as fast as you can. Understand?"

"Yeah, sure." This didn't bode well. George didn't know what these guys were up to, but he was pretty sure they weren't looking for legal advice. Christoff threw him the keys and walked away with The Shrew in tow.

George exhaled a long, nervous breath. Maybe infiltrating the mob wasn't such a great idea after all; there had to be an easier way for a reporter to break out. He shimmied across the front bench seat and settled in behind the wheel. What were Christoff and his buddy doing at a law firm? If they were just here for a meeting, why did they need George for a quick getaway? From his limited criminal experience, law firms weren't the kind of place typically used to make drug deals, and he couldn't imagine them shaking down lawyers for money. Lawyers were their own kind of sharks.

Trying to calm himself, he turned his thoughts to Pashmina. Just thinking about her made him happy. He loved her so much it was impossible to imagine his life without her, and thankfully he would never have to. She may have said she loved Harry but she was in love with George. Why else would she have stayed with him all this time? That was the crux of it, and that's what he had told Harry. A twinge of guilt went through George briefly as he recalled his emotional power play to get Harry out of the picture. Maybe it was a little selfish of him, but he wouldn't lose any sleep worrying about it. It was for the best.

George's head banged against the window as the back door opened with a ferocity that rocked the car. In a flurry, something was thrust into the back. The Shrew jumped into the front seat and screamed at George, "Let's go! Go! Go!"

Instinctively, George turned the key and floored it, racing away from the building and avoiding the main streets. "Where am I going?" he asked frantically, not daring to look in the rear view mirror.

"Head to the port," The Shrew instructed. "There's a building just before you get to the docks. It's a machine shop for marine equipment. Pull in and park around back."

They raced along the streets of Piraeus, George's knuckles clenched tight around the steering wheel, beads of sweat forming on his upper lip. Just outside the city limits he slowed his speed, as no one seemed to be chasing them, and he wasn't going to do anything to call attention to them. Relaxing slightly, he glanced quickly in the rearview mirror towards the back seat.

Christoff was lying across it holding down a male figure. He had his arm around the man's neck and was struggling to pull a cloth bag over his head. The man, who appeared to be much smaller than Christoff, was pushing against the seat trying to break free. With a closed fist, Christoff punched him in the head repeatedly until he stopped struggling then covered his head and bound his wrists together with twine.

George began to shake uncontrollably. What the hell was happening? Obviously the guy wasn't there of his own volition. "Shit! Shit! Shit!" he cursed silently. "What the fuck have I gotten into?"

He stole a quick glance at The Shrew who was staring straight ahead at the road. Calm, cool and collected, the guy was so nonchalant he seemed bored. George felt sick.

They were about ten minutes away from the port, and George's mind raced desperately as he tried to figure out what to do. Dumbass, what have you gotten yourself into? He took a deep breath and tried to infuse some common sense into his terror. This was a giant fucking mistake, but he'd be fine. His editor knew what he was up to and would help *if he could*. He would vouch for George, and proclaim his innocence in all this crap *if George lived that long.*

He glanced in the rearview again. Things were relatively quiet back there where the little man was still subdued. George breathed deeply and focused on driving. A few minutes later The Shrew pointed to the left. "Right there, that's the building. Pull in here and go around back."

The car screeched as George made a quick turn into the vacant parking lot and pulled up to a nondescript warehouse void of any discernible markings. His heart sank to the pit of his stomach. If things got out of hand, and he was pretty sure now they would, he was up a creek. No one knew he was here, and no one would ever find him. He felt a sudden kinship with the hooded one in his back seat. George and the little man were goners.

Pulling in close to the back of the building, he parked the car and glanced over at The Shrew who was already opening the passenger door. "Get out," he said quietly to George. Taking the keys out of the ignition, George's hand shook as he placed them in his pocket and waited outside the car for further instructions.

Christoff emerged, dragging the little man, and shoved him towards the building where The Shrew and George waited beside a small open door. Inside, George looked anxiously around the space. It was empty. Only a carpet of aged machine oil spots covering the concrete floor and grime-covered windows providing privacy with the effectiveness of a roman shade, gave proof of a business abandoned long ago.

Christoff entered, alternately dragging and shoving the little man along. His head still covered with a bag, the prisoner stumbled and fell to the floor with a yelp. Instinctively, George moved to help him, but The Shrew reached him first, punching him savagely in the head. The little man screamed and coiled in a fetal position.

Christoff scolded his partner. "Jesus, let's just get on with it. Get him to give us the information, and let's be done with this."

The Shrew pulled the bag off the little man's head and George stared, unable to look away. The man's face was covered in sweat, his eyes were crazed, filled with terror like a trapped animal, and bruises were already forming on his punch bag of a face. He looked frantically back and forth between Christoff and The Shrew, glancing briefly at George who shrugged sympathetically. *I don't know any more than you do, buddy.*

Leaning in, The Shrew pinned the man with a snake-like gaze, cold and unblinking, then kicked the little man soundly in the torso, eliciting a cry of pain. "What the hell do you want from me, you piece of shit?"

The Shrew pulled back his arm to strike again, but Christoff intercepted him. "Enough! Let's get this done."

George stayed quiet, watching the drama unfold like a TV crime show. What exactly was happening here? A robbery? Extortion? Kidnapping?

Suddenly emboldened, the little man spoke. "Tell me what the hell you want from me," he demanded. "My associates know I'm missing. They'll alert the police."

The Shrew chuckled unpleasantly. "I don't think so, my friend. And even if they do, you'll be in a dozen pieces all over this floor before they find you."

Christoff glared at The Shrew before turning to look at their quarry. "You know why you're here, Vargos. You failed to deliver what you promised and made the family look foolish. That's not good."

At the mention of the word 'family,' Vargos paled. Suddenly Vargos and Christoff and The Shrew were all on the same page. George looked from one to the next fascinated.

"I did what I could!" Vargos asserted, "I can't buy the courts. The decision was out of my hands."

Christoff's chuckle rang hollow without a smile to keep it company. "Vargos, you took our money and promised you'd take care of the courts. But you didn't." He looked almost sad. "And now someone has to pay the price." He took two steps toward Vargos who was hopelessly struggling to protect himself, his bound hands more hindrance than help. "Tell us who is responsible. We know someone swayed the court. Who was it? All we need is a name."

Vargos blinked in disbelief. George was skeptical. That was all they wanted? The Shrew stepped closer to Vargos, and without warning landed a kick to his lower back. Vargos screamed in pain and tried to cover his head. Undeterred, The Shrew punched him again, slamming his fist into Vargos' head as thick red blood splattered like paint on the canvas of the oil-spotted floor.

Vargos wasn't screaming anymore. He was slumped on the floor unconscious and George was scared. Vargos had broken a promise to the wrong people and now he would be lucky if he survived this 'little chat.' And what about George, what about his role in all of this? Just because he wasn't the one throwing the punches, didn't mean the authorities would care about that. He was an accomplice. Or worse, a scapegoat for Christoff and The Shrew. Either way he was screwed.

George was all alone with no one to protect him. He had to get out of here now. Discreetly patting his pocket for the car keys, he checked to make sure his buddies' attention was focused on their captive and began inching his way quietly towards the door.

Christoff was hovering over Vargos, waiting for some sign of life, while The Shrew paced back and forth flexing his bruised knuckles and fingers. George didn't wait for an engraved invitation. He bolted for the exit, pulling the keys from his pocket as he went. Sprinting through the door, he raced towards the car and jumped in, jamming the lock down behind him.

Almost immediately the warehouse door flew open again and The Shrew flew out like a heat-seeking missile. He spotted George instantly. With trembling hands, George turned the key, roaring the car to life. Yes! Throwing it into drive he hit the gas just as The Shrew threw himself onto the hood, arms and legs splayed, his eyes boring bullet holes through the windshield. George was a dead man.

Slamming his foot on the brake, George tried to shake him, but The Shrew hung on biding his time. For a moment they stared at each other and George started trembling again as the other man sneered confidently. He was going to enjoy shooting George in the head. George hit the gas, looking for speed, lots of it and fast before he swung the wheel sideways sending the car into a spiral spin.

The Shrew flew off like a kite, and George sped away not bothering to see if he was alive or not. He didn't care. He sped out into the road and drove blindly. "Get away. Get the fuck away!" he screamed loudly, his eyes darting repeatedly to the rearview mirror.

He drove, putting distance between him and the disaster he had left behind until he could breathe again, then scanned the road for somewhere safe to hide. Slowing in front of a small café, he pulled the car deep into the bowels of an adjacent alley where darkness completely obscured it from the road.

George entered the café which was pleasantly humming with sounds of business; waiters and patrons chatting quietly, glasses clinking, and the occasional burst of laughter created a muted balm that soothed his highly frazzled nerves. This was exactly the kind of safe haven he needed, his temporary oasis until he could get his shit together.

He headed towards the bar, motioning the bartender over as he went. "A phone." He spoke calmly, only a slight quiver hinting at his inner panic. "I need to use a phone. Quickly, please."

The bartender looked him over and nodded his head towards the back of the café. "Back there."

The manager's office was at the end of a dark hallway just past the restrooms. Spotting the shiny black phone, George closed the door behind him and dialed quickly, waiting impatiently for someone to answer.

"Hello?" a male voice answered gruffly.

The familiar voice was comforting and George's knees buckled. He grabbed the desk for support. He wasn't home free yet.

"Troy. Listen carefully. I need you to come get me *right now*." A frenzied stream of questions came over the line but George cut them off. "I'll explain everything when I see you, just get here, fast." He gave his location and hung up, collapsing into a chair while he waited for help to arrive.

A half hour later, the door opened slowly and George held his breath, terrified, until he saw a familiar head pop around it. Air started filling his lungs again. "Thank God it's you."

Troy took stock of his usually happy-go-lucky brother with growing alarm. George was a shaking mass of nerves, and it scared the hell out of him too. They had to get out of here. Now. Wasting no time, he grabbed his brother by the arm, "Let's go, I'm parked out front." Glued to his seat, George didn't budge. "I said, let's go!" Troy barked, snapping George to attention.

Grabbing Troy, George stood and pulled him close, squeezing his younger brother tightly. "You saved my life."

"Not unless we move…now!" Grabbing George's arm, he pulled him towards the door.

* * *

Tim was almost prone across the table not wanting to miss a softly-spoken word of George's incredible story. Fucking unbelievable.

"So what happened to Vargos?"

"What happened to Vargos is the reason I disappeared," George answered. "Troy took me back to his place for a few days until I could make sense of things. We figured it would be okay for a little while at least. Christoff didn't know my real name, only my alias, Nichos Copulous."

"Then a day or so later I heard a news report that a high profile lawyer named Vargos Nos was dead. His body had been found on the shore of Piraeus…stuffed in pieces in a metal drum, his decapitated head sitting on top of the drum like a calling card."

A soft whistle escaped Tim's lips. "They murdered him?"

"The Adelphos is serious business. Whatever it was that Vargos didn't deliver became his death sentence."

"What did you do then?" Tim asked.

"Well, even though Christoff didn't know my real name, I was scared. I felt like it was only a matter of time before they found me. Every minute I stayed, put me and everyone I loved, my family, your mother in grave danger. So Troy and I came up with a plan to smuggle me out of the country. After that I spent years traveling the world, doing odd jobs to get by and keeping a low profile until I thought it was safe to go home again." He shrugged, signaling the end of his story. "I've been in Cronilys ever since."

From the sounds of it, George had led a lonely life. Tim empathized. "What about my mother? Did you ever see her again?"

George pondered the question, answering slowly. "No…and yes. A few days before I was supposed to leave, I asked her to meet me so I could explain everything that was happening and ask her to wait for me. But before that happened there was a report of another body found. This time it was Christoff. He'd been murdered and left in an alley next to a police station."

"Christoff, too?" Tim was stunned.

"Yes, they left his body so close to the police station it was almost as if they were daring the authorities to intervene. In some ways, I actually felt relieved. Now the only person who knew of my involvement was The Shrew. But he was the most dangerous of all and I knew I had to leave immediately."

"I missed my date with your mother, and I didn't contact her again. I thought it would be too dangerous for both of us. By the time I was ready, so many years had passed I figured she had her own life and didn't need me intruding on it. I never stopped loving her, but I wasn't sure if I could make her happy anymore."

His voice cracked and George took a sip of his drink. "But that's still not the end of the story," he smiled brightly. "A year ago, maybe a little longer, I ran into your mother when she was home visiting her family. We had a wonderful time reminiscing and catching up. I even started to hope we might get back together, but she blew my proposal out of the water."

He looked so sheepish Tim couldn't help but laugh. "Uh oh, what'd you do?"

"It's more like what I did and didn't do." Shaking his head in disgust, "What's the saying? Women, you can't live with them, you can't live without them."

Tim nodded, understanding. "I've got a girlfriend too."

George's bushy brows spiked upward. It was small, but Tim was starting to open up. "My mistake was thinking I knew what was best for her; I told her husband about us. He wasn't happy but he believed, like me, that she'd be happier with me than him and he left her. But your mother felt differently, I guess, and to top it off she never knew why he left. He never told her about our talk and neither did I."

"And that, as they say, is the rest of the story." Raising his glass in mock toast, George took a sip, savoring the taste and feel of the cool liquid gliding down his throat. "When she heard what I did all those years ago, she was furious and stormed off. We haven't spoken since."

Tim's stomach lurched making him queasy. He had learned so much tonight, but there was still one thing he had to know. "Are you ready to tell me who my mother is?"

George's face creased instantly with worry. If he knew his son even a little bit, just her name wouldn't be enough. Tim would want more and he deserved more, but George didn't have it to give. How pathetic. He had been a father for less than twenty-four hours and he was already failing his kid. That had to be some kind of record.

"I wish I could tell you more," George faltered before spilling what he knew. "Your mother came to Boston right before you were born and has been here ever since. She's a novelist, well-known, popular worldwide and her name," he paused, dragging air into his tight chest, "is Pashmina Papadakis."

Tim barely heard him, still fixated on a single point; his mother lived here in the same city he did, where he had grown up, gone to college, where he worked, where he walked and ate at restaurants. Maybe they had already crossed paths. Maybe he had held a door open for her, or waited behind her in the Starbucks line.

Wait. "What?" Tim asked, dazed.

George repeated his question. "Pashmina, have you heard of her?"

His mother was Pashmina Papadakis. Pashmina Papadakis was his mother. This was insane on so many levels. He grabbed his glass, knocking it back like a shot, and signaled the waitress to bring another round. "Of course I've heard of her, hasn't everybody? You're telling me that you had an affair with Pashmina Papadakis?"

"She wasn't famous when I was with her, but yes, we were involved."

"And she gave me up because she was young and alone," Tim mused, crunching on an ice cube. "I get that. But then why wouldn't she look for me later, when she could afford to take care of herself and me?"

His wounded eyes welled with tears, breaking George's heart into tiny pieces. "I wish I knew."

CHAPTER TWELVE

Glancing furtively at Amelia sleeping beside him, Tim pinched himself on the arm and blushed. His childish behavior was really embarrassing but he couldn't help it. So much had happened lately, he needed a reality check to make sure he wasn't dreaming.

In a few weeks he would be joining the rank and file of Brown Books as their new Vice President of Marketing. Despite getting off to a rocky start, he and Chad had managed to overcome their differences and questionable opinions of each other to see the benefits of collaborating professionally. With Chad's name and business acumen, and Tim's savvy knowhow and pit bull tenacity, they would knock the publishing world on its competitive little ass. That's what Chad had said, sounding totally unlike the silver spoon baby Tim had always pegged him for. This was 'tough guy' Chad, and Tim kind of liked him.

And then there was George. His dad. It still sounded strange to Tim even after their whirlwind reunion, but he wasn't complaining. It couldn't have been easy for George either, discovering he was a father and had been for twenty-nine years, but he seemed to take it in stride. George had taken a huge risk sharing the truth of his checkered past with Tim. "I've made a lot of mistakes and hurt a lot of people in my life, but I really hope I haven't totally scared you off. More than anything I just want to be a part of your life."

No, George wasn't perfect, but he was a good man and that was enough for Tim. They focused on building a father/son relationship they could both live with, one that satisfied both George's newfound paternal interests and Tim's inherent independence. His mother was another story, however, not to mention 'the elephant in the airport' as George readied to fly home.

George felt helpless that he couldn't do more to reunite Tim and Pashmina. A boy, even one twenty-nine years old needed his mother and Pashmina was his mother even if she wasn't acting like it. Placing a firm hand on Tim's shoulder, George said, "I wish I could be with you when you meet Pashmina. She's beautiful and independent and head-strong, and you're a lot like her." Tim's eyes grew wide with surprise and George chuckled. "Go easy on her. I'm sure she has her reasons for doing what she did."

"Frowning already? It's not even 7:00 o'clock yet." Amelia's voice pulled Tim back to the present. She yawned and stretched, pulling herself up beside Tim. "Bet I can put a smile back on your handsome face." She kissed him, gently at first, then deeply, her tongue artfully probing the warmth of his mouth until her pulse raced and Tim's breathing quickened. Groaning with pleasure, he pulled her on top of him, the silky strands of her hair enveloping them both like the boughs of a weeping willow, soft and sheltering. Tim forgot about his parents, his new job, and everything else for a while.

"Told you I could make you smile," Amelia teased later.

"I didn't doubt it for a minute." He kissed her forehead, pushed himself out of bed, and headed for the bathroom.

Smoothing the rumpled bed covers around her, Amelia spoke to the open doorway in what she hoped was a casual tone. "So you've been having quite the week," she started. "A new job. Congratulations again, Mr. Vice President of Marketing at Brown Books." A muffled thanks floated back to her. "Then meeting your biological father. That's huge."

"Mmm hmm. Huge."

"You must be on Cloud 9."

"Maybe even 10," he joked, wiping the remains of his morning shave from his face.

"We should celebrate."

"Definitely."

"Great!" Amelia beamed like a kid on Christmas morning. "I have an idea. Now I know after our first date we promised no more work functions, but," she took a nervous breath and let the rest of her words spill out, "I have this thing tonight. It's kind of business, but not really because Uncle Monte will be there too, and he's not business, he's family." Was she babbling? She was babbling. "Anyway, the point is I'm having dinner tonight with him and Pashmina Papadakis. They're old friends, and Pashmina and I are becoming friends, and Uncle Monte and me, well, you know." Her voice trailed off quietly.

She paused, and hearing nothing from the bathroom, continued. "Pashmina and I have been working around the clock on her book getting it ready for deadline and we're feeling a little burnt. We need something to recharge us." Amelia paused, the twisted sheet was like a Twizzler between her hands. "She suggested a double date, her and Monte and you and me. It's perfect."

Crickets. "And it's the perfect way to launch your new career in publishing, having dinner with one of the greatest fiction writers of our time," she said, sweetening the pot, "I mean that's something even Chadwick Brown would kill for. So what do you think?" Amelia was ready to beg. "Will you bend the 'no business rule' for me this once?"

Standing in front of the bathroom mirror, his palms resting on the edge of the sink, Tim considered his astonished expression staring back at him. You've gotta be shitting me, was she serious? Pashmina was all he had been thinking about since George had encouraged him to find her. *"You're a lot like her."*

He thought about the collection of Pashmina Papadakis mystery novels on the book shelf in Amelia's room. While she had made them dinner and chatted with Rose, catching up on the dirt of the day, he had inspected them like a thief, glancing over his shoulder to avoid being caught. Every book was the same, with an ornate front cover illustration and a portrait of Pashmina on the back sitting erect, hands elegantly crossed in her lap and a Mona Lisa smile flitting about her lips. Admittedly, they shared more than a passing resemblance as well as an incredible secret he couldn't wait to reveal.

"Sure," he called out to Amelia.

"Sure?" She couldn't believe it. "That's it, 'sure,' no begging or pleading required?"

Poking his head through the doorway, Tim flashed his most heart-melting smile. She had no idea the gift she had just given him. "Not this time. In fact, I owe you one."

"How do you figure?" Amelia flopped back on the pillows in relief.

"So you've forgotten our first date already?"

"Not forgotten, just forgiven. Let's call it even. Agreed?"

"Agreed." Feeling like he had dodged a bullet, Tim stepped into the shower and let the steady stream of droplets pelt down on him. He knew he should have told Amelia the truth about Pashmina, but he couldn't. Scratch that, he didn't want to, not yet. Even the nervous bubbles suddenly flitting around in his stomach like a just-opened bottle of seltzer didn't lessen his desire to stay quiet. Suddenly he couldn't wait to meet Pashmina, and a crazy calm took over as he imagined an outburst of tearful hugs and loving words bringing them together again. He was happy just thinking about it, and he wanted to keep it that way, his dream unspoiled and untouched by anyone else.

Through the shower door he saw Amelia examining herself in the mirror, searching for imperfections in her flawless face. He knew how she felt. "Stop worrying," he called out to her, wondering who he was really trying to convince, "you're perfect just the way you are."

* * *

Street lights danced and twinkled like so many fireflies flitting about the warm summer night as darkness settled over the Boston Public Gardens. From inside the restaurant, Pashmina gazed at the view and sighed contentedly. Beautiful.

Beside her Monte tipped his drink in a toast, "To a lovely evening and an even more beautiful woman."

Pashmina smiled warmly, touching her glass to his. Thank God for Monte. From their first meeting as two greenhorns at a small publishing house till now, he had been her dearest friend besides Sofie, standing by her through thick and thin, sharing her secrets, and lending a manly shoulder to lean on when she needed it. Theirs was a deep and loving friendship, friends with benefits as the youth of today would say, minus all the trappings of a committed relationship. After Harry, Pashmina had never wanted to commit herself to any other man; Monte understood that and accepted it without question.

Sipping his drink, he winked flirtatiously at Pashmina, eliciting a girlish giggle from her. She watched him fondly, taking note of his long slender fingers wrapped gently but protectively around his glass the same way he often held her hand; this man was her rock, strong and dependable, with a snow-cap of soft white hair and a matching mustache, neatly trimmed. He cut a dashing figure in his hand-crafted Italian silk suit, like an older version of James Bond, but equally debonair and a man of mystery as well. "I can't believe in all the years we've known each other I've never met Amelia until now. I mean, I knew you had a niece in Boston, but you've kept her well hidden."

"It's not something I'm very proud of, I'm afraid," Monte replied, eliciting a look of shock. "Oh, don't get me wrong, Amelia's a lovely girl, the daughter I never had really," he explained. "I was ecstatic when she decided to attend college in Boston. For me and her. You see, her mother, my sister Francesca, has a tendency to suffocate the ones she loves most with her attention and devotion, but Amelia's too independent for that kind of love, she wanted to make her own way in the world."

He sighed. "Francesca only agreed to let her come after I promised to look out for her while she was here." He looked at Pashmina sheepishly. "But I'm afraid I did that a bit too well for my sister's liking."

"What do you mean?"

"Well, while she was still in school, I arranged for Amelia to intern at Dewes. At the time, she didn't really have a career focus of any kind but she's smart, and sharp, and dedicated, and I just figured working at Dewes would be fun for her, give her some extra spending money, that sort of thing. But the crazy girl fell in love with publishing, and Dewes loved her and offered her a full-time position after she graduated. Needless to say, she stayed up North a long way from home and her mother in South Carolina; Francesca blames me for that."

He smiled sadly, swirling his drink so the ice cubes bounced off one another like bumper cars. "Francesca's not really mad at me, I know that, but I feel guilty all the same. If anyone did anything--intentional or otherwise--to keep my child away from me, I wouldn't be happy either."

A shadow passed fleetingly over Pashmina's face, and Monte hurried to comfort her. "I'm sorry, Darling. I didn't mean to remind you of your own loss."

"It's all right," she assured him, "you didn't remind me of anything I don't think about all the time anyway."

Monte nodded sympathetically.

"Okay, no more sadness tonight," Pashmina said, smiling brightly. "Tonight is about having fun, spending time with good people, and stuffing ourselves with delicious food."

"I'm in, but I hope Amelia and Tim get here soon because I'm starving!"

* * *

"There they are," said Amelia, pointing to Pashmina and Monte chatting quietly together at a table. Claiming a ticket from the cloak room clerk, Tim moved to stand beside Amelia, his eyes following the direction of her gaze.

"They're a striking couple," he observed, though he only had eyes for Pashmina. Her raven hair gleamed sleekly in the candlelight, and rosy spots of color blossomed on her smooth olive cheeks as she blushed prettily under Monte's admiring attention. Ever so slightly, Tim raised his eyes to meet hers, two almonds dipped in rich dark chocolate just like his.

There she was, his lovely mother, looking directly at him. She didn't look like the kind of person who would heartlessly abandon her baby. Hope trumped hurt as Tim's heart pounded. Pashmina's eyes lit up, flickering with excitement. Smiling, she waved him over. Did she recognize him? Tim started to raise his arm in response, but Amelia grabbed it and squeezed his hand. "You ready? C'mon, they're waiting for us."

Monte and Pashmina stood to greet them as they approached the table and Tim waited impatiently as Amelia hugged first Pashmina and then her uncle. Then it was his turn.

"Uncle Monte, you remember Tim, don't you?" she asked as the two shook hands.

"And, Pashmina, I'd like to introduce you to my boyfriend, Timothy Smith. Don't hold it against him, but Tim just joined Brown Books as their new VP of Marketing," she announced proudly.

"That's wonderful," Pashmina congratulated Tim, kissing him gently on both cheeks. "We must celebrate, don't you think Monte? How about some champagne?"

Reluctant to let her go, Tim continued to grasp Pashmina by the arms, savoring her perfumed scent and the tingling sensation where her lips had touched his skin. "I'm afraid I'm not much of a champagne man," he apologized.

"No?" Pashmina eyed him head to toe. Leaning towards him conspiratorially, she whispered, "To tell you the truth, neither am I, it gives me a terrible hangover; what about a nice gin and tonic instead?" He nodded and let a laughing Pashmina lead him to the table. "Come on then, let's get this party started!"

* * *

Tim felt like an outsider, looking into a transparent bubble where the others laughed and talked easily while he sat quietly, present but not engaged. Aside from the occasional worried glance from Amelia, no one even seemed to notice as he watched and listened, studying Pashmina's every movement, from the elegant turn of her head as she spoke to Monte and Amelia, to the graceful arch of her brows lifting up and down in delight.

Tim had imagined this moment all day, the moment when he and his mother would finally meet, and he still didn't know what to do or say. *Hi, I'm Tim, your son.* To the point but not very smooth. He grimaced. Maybe he shouldn't say anything just yet, maybe he should just try to get to know her a little bit first. As much as he wanted to just blurt it out right now, he was too scared. Curbing his impatience, he decided to relax and join the conversation.

As their waiter cleared the table, Tim addressed Pashmina. "I have a few weeks off before I start at Brown, and I'm thinking of taking a vacation, maybe to Greece."

"Really?" Amelia turned to him in surprise. "How long have you been thinking about this?"

"Not long," he shot her a meaningful glance. "What do you think, Pashmina?"

"Next to here, Greece is my favorite place on Earth," she beamed, "and I think it would be even if I hadn't been born and raised there."

"So why did you leave?" Inquiring minds wanted to know, or at least he did.

"Some things are beyond our control," she said simply. "I came here because I had to, but I've never regretted it for a minute."

"When did you come here exactly?"

"Oh, a long, long time ago. 1979. Back then I was tall, thin and blonde," she joked. Used to admiring glances from men, Pashmina couldn't help but notice Tim hadn't taken his eyes off her all night.

"That's what Tim always says!" Amelia chimed in, squeezing his hand affectionately. "He's always teasing me and his friend Ben that blondes have more fun, but I'll take his dark swarthy looks any day."

Pashmina considered him through slit eyes. "Mmm, you do have a bit of the bad boy look about you," she teased, turning his skin bright red, "maybe even a little Mediterranean coloring. Where are your parents from?"

Tim felt like a bug under a microscope. The question caught him off guard. "Tim's adopted," Amelia answered, misinterpreting his silence for embarrassment.

Pashmina smiled and reached to touch his hand gently with her own. "I've always admired people who become parents to children without any of their own. You must feel very blessed."

At that moment, whatever thoughts Tim had had about what would happen when he finally met his mother, went out the wide-paned window beside him. Feeling like a bucket of water had slapped him in the face, Tim was stunned. WTF? Was she really that callous, or was it just an 'out of sight, out mind' mentality that erased the guilt of giving up her own baby?

He snorted derisively. "Is that what you call it? You think I'm blessed that my real mother didn't think I was good enough to hold on to? Or, maybe I'm just blessed because she gave me to an adoption agency instead of ditching me on a doorstep somewhere." Tim's head was pounding with a bitter resentment he hadn't expected and couldn't control. He had to get out of here, now, before the train completely derailed.

Pashmina was a statue in her seat. Through all the years she had mourned the loss of her child, her only comfort was the fervent belief that her baby was safe and part of a loving family. How could anyone feel unloved and rejected by parents that were good and kind?

Silence stretched between them as Pashmina collected her thoughts and Tim struggled to contain his emotions. Amelia stared at him speechless and wide-eyed from behind her water glass, as Monte cleared his throat repeatedly, their actions speaking to Tim louder than words: 'fix this'.

But he couldn't, not here, not now, not after that awful outburst. "I'll go get our coats," he said to Amelia. "Thank you for dinner," he nodded to Monte, then let his eyes light on Pashmina one last time. "I'm sorry for snapping at you. It's been a long week and I've got a lot on my mind. I hope you'll forgive me."

Unable to speak, Pashmina nodded good-bye, tears welling inexplicably in her eyes as she watched him leave the room. A few minutes ago she had felt trapped by his endless questions and piercing gaze, now he was gone and all she wanted to do was run after him and bring him back. And she hadn't the slightest idea why.

CHAPTER THIRTEEN

Tim waited, one foot tapping impatiently, for the elevator to reach the lobby only three floors down. "C'mon," he commanded, slamming his hand on the wall of the slow-moving cubicle, "I don't have all day." As if on cue, the elevator came to a halt, its shiny doors barely sliding open before Tim raced through them, startling Ben who was waiting calmly on the other side.

"Whoa, where's the fire?" He grabbed Tim's arms, steadying them both. "Wait, it's Saturday, right?"

Tim snorted, taking in Ben's disheveled appearance. Wearing yesterday's suit, the jacket carelessly slung over one shoulder, a golden shadow on his unshaven face, and a bed-head of tousled curls, Ben looked like a teddy bear heading home from a night of lovin' at the Jamboree. "Well, well, Mr. Morning After. How're we feeling today?"

"Like a million bucks," Ben grinned, jokingly flexing his biceps, "Ready for anything."

"Great, then do me a favor and take care of Amelia for me while I'm out."

"What do you mean?"

Tim snuck a glance at his watch. "Look, I don't have time to explain right now, but Amelia's totally pissed at me and she's on her way over to let me have it."

"And you're leaving?" Ben watched in disbelief as Tim headed for the front door. "Dude, you can't do that. You can't do that to Amelia, you can't do that to me!" he shouted as the revolving door turned like a windmill, shooing Tim out of sight.

Dodging and weaving his way through the busy city streets, his mind focused on one thing only, Tim barely noticed the Saturday morning crowds. He had to see Pashmina right away and make up for last night's disaster. He winced. So much for taking George's advice to cut her some slack. Contrary to having the upper hand, being the only one 'in the know' about Pashmina's identity was proving to be a real disadvantage.

"There are two sides to every story," Ben had once said, explaining his winning courtroom strategy, "and somewhere in the middle lies the truth." Well, Tim knew his story, lived it and didn't much like it. Blaming the mother who had forced it all on him was only natural. But if he was honest with himself there was more to the story than just what he knew, and he owed Pashmina the chance to explain. He owed himself the chance to hear it.

* * *

Amelia knocked heavily on the door of Tim's apartment, the hearty rap of her knuckles sounding like a battering ram to her self-conscious ears. Silence. Praying the neighbors wouldn't notice, she bombarded the door with another rapid fire volley. Did he seriously go back to sleep after her blasting phone call earlier? She pounded on the door again.

"Just a minute! Ouch, ow!"A moment later, the door swung open, inviting her to enter.

"Hey!" Ben called from the small galley-style kitchen. Poking his head around the corner, he smiled and waved at her. "Come in, come in. Sorry to leave you hanging out there, I just had a small emergency." He stepped out of the kitchen, a bath towel wrapped round his waist, a blood-soaked dish towel pressed firmly against his neck.

Amelia blanched. "Oh my God, what happened?" Ignoring his protests, she gently peeled the cloth from his skin, revealing an elongated strip of coagulating blood underneath. She whistled softly, tracing the tip of her finger down its narrow length. "Impressive. Turbo blade or regular?" she teased. Ben scowled.

She laughed, "Well, it was close, but I think you'll live. You might want think about some shaving lessons before you try it again, though."

"Thanks for the diagnoses and the tip." With a mocking bow Ben continued, "Now if you'll excuse me for a minute, I'm going to finish washing up and put some clothes on."

"No problem. Hey, send Tim out here will you?" she called after him.

Cursing silently, he turned back to apologize, "He's not here right now."

Amelia exhaled, not even realizing she had been holding her breath. Somewhere deep inside she had known he wouldn't be here. It was his MO not to be around when it mattered most, but it still didn't hurt any less. And on top of that, now she was confused, too. What the hell happened last night? Rude didn't begin to describe Tim's awful behavior.

Ben fidgeted awkwardly, uncertain what to do. Amelia might have laughed at his discomfort, except she knew exactly how he felt. "When did he leave?" she asked, plopping disheartened on the couch.

"A while ago." He moved to join her. Lost in their own thoughts, they sat half listening to the sounds of the day drifting lazily in through the open window. When a raspy chorus of blaring horns broke the lull, Ben asked, "What do you want to do?"

Amelia turned her head to look at him, leaning comfortably back against the cushions. "What I really want to do is slap him and say 'what the fuck's wrong with you, why are you always such an asshole?' " She shook her head and laughed. "But my mother, who is a wise and wonderful woman, and by the way would never believe I'm saying nice things about her, always says that there are two sides to every story."

"So you're saying there's a good reason Tim's an asshole?"

Amelia laughed again. "I don't know about a *good* reason, but yeah, there must be some explanation. So I guess I'll just wait for him to come back and enlighten me."

"This should be good," Ben said, heading towards the kitchen. "In the meantime how about some breakfast?"

* * *

From where he stood across the street, Tim could see Pashmina moving gracefully about the living room, organizing a few magazines here, shifting a chair there, adjusting the drapes that framed the over-sized windows. Spotting him, her eyes widened and her busy hands stilled, clinging to the fabric for support. For a moment, they watched each other, wary, suspicious, until Pashmina blinked and stepping away from the window, moved out of his sight.

Squaring his shoulders, Tim marched purposefully up the front steps just as she opened the door.

"Well, this is a surprise," Pashmina said dryly, "I didn't expect to see you again. Did you forget something, another hurtful remark or an insult, maybe?"

Wondering if he deserved such animosity, and deciding he did after his dinner time tantrum, Tim apologized, "I behaved badly last night. I'm sorry. But if you'll give me a few minutes to explain, I think you'll understand why."

Still guarded, Pashmina searched his face intently for some clue to why he was there. Not even a shadow of last night's dark display lingered in the bright sweetness of his boyish features. A minute passed and then another as she struggled to control her growing curiosity. Who was she kidding? She never could resist a good mystery. "Come in," she invited at last.

They walked together through the front foyer and down a short hallway into a cozy room Tim recognized as the site of Pashmina's earlier tidying. Now inside, he could see it was impeccably neat except for a large desk topped with a computer, reams of paper stacked in piles of varying height, a coffee mug full of pens and pencils, and a small pewter picture frame, back turned as if hiding its contents from the rest of the room.

"So this is where the magic happens," he observed, casually making his way over to the desk. He pointed to the piles of papers, "Is this what you and Amelia are working on?"

Pashmina started to reply then stopped, watching nervously as he picked up the frame from her desk and studied it for a long moment. "Is this you and...?"

"Me and my husband," she answered, taking the frame and carefully returning it to its place of honor next to her computer. How many times had she lost herself in the memories of this photo? Harry, so young and handsome in his uniform, standing with his arm draped protectively around her sun kissed shoulders as she clasped both her arms tightly around his waist, the summer wind teasing her long hair like Medusa's head and making them both laugh out loud. "He'd just returned from a nine-month detail." She smiled, remembering. "We were so happy he was home."

"His name was Harry?"

She stared sharply. "Yes, it was. How did you know?"

With a final glance at the smiling couple, Tim settled comfortably on an elegantly appointed Louis XIV sofa with silk cushions the same ice blue color of Amelia's eyes. She was probably at his place right now bending Ben's ear about last night, but Tim couldn't worry about that right now, he had some talking of his own to do.

"My dad told me." The full weight of her attention fell on him, and he was thankful to be sitting down. "My biological dad, that is. I just met him for the first time." He smiled, it still felt so good. "He didn't even know I existed until recently, but then he hired a private investigator to find me."

Mesmerized, Pashmina watched with growing unease as his widespread fingers slid smoothly through waves of dark, silky hair like a swimmer gliding through water, reminding her of someone else.

"Can you imagine," he said with almost childish wonder, "twenty-nine years old and I just met my dad for the first time? Out of the blue, BAM! There he was in my office."

Her mouth too dry to speak above the roar of blood rushing through her ears, Pashmina smiled weakly as Tim explained.

"You know, all I've ever wanted was to know who my real parents are. Of course I've tried to find them, too, but this was so much better. He found me."

"I'm happy for you," she said, her voice cracking like a pubescent boy's, her eyes drinking him in, his face suddenly as familiar as her own. "So, is he in Boston? Does he live around here?"

Their eyes locked knowingly. "No," Tim spoke softly, choosing his words carefully, still holding her gaze with his own. He licked his dry lips nervously. This was hard but he was tired of beating around the bush. Time to come clean. "George is from Greece, like you. George Levendakis is my father, and…"

"I'm your mother." Self-propelled, the words flew from her lips, surprising them both, and floated weightlessly around her. For one interminable moment, neither one moved, frozen in place by her startled admission until a sob burst from Pashmina's chest breaking the spell.

"You're my son," she whispered, drinking him in like a woman dying of thirst. It was so obvious; his eyes were exact replicas of hers, his strong and square jaw could have been chiseled from the same block of marble, and a cool reserve that covered his thoughts and emotions like frost on a windowpane was a mask she herself had perfected. How did she not see it before? "You're my son."

Instinctively she moved to hug him, to hold him, relief flooding through her as his nervous tension eased, and he gradually relaxed in her embrace. She held him tighter, reluctant to let him go, surprised at how natural it felt to have him in her arms again after twenty-nine years. She had never stopped loving him. She had never stopped being his mother in spirit if not in fact. He had to know that. Shifting slightly, she raised her hands, her fingers dancing lightly over his face, the proud Grecian nose and the sculpted planes of his cheeks smudged with the sharp stubble of five o'clock shadow, a painful reminder of the childhood she had missed. Her baby boy was gone, replaced by this fine young man.

"I never thought I'd see you again," she whispered, reluctantly releasing him from her hold. "I can't believe it."

"Me neither." Suddenly lost for words, Tim fidgeted nervously on the couch and cleared his throat. What now?

"When I was with George he told me what he knew, his version of what happened, why he never knew about me." Afraid to say more, he dropped his head and prayed she would understand his silent plea.

"You want to know my story." It was a statement, not a question, and it was a vulnerable little boy, not her grown son nodding at her affirmatively.

"You're a lot like him, you know," she smiled at Tim sitting quietly, his eyes glued on her. "Your mannerisms, your gestures, and handsome. George was always so handsome."

She sighed deeply. "He was such a dear friend and I cared for him a great deal but he was also arrogant and selfish and he overstepped his bounds with me." Storm clouds darkened her pensive face. George had had no business talking to Harry, no right, and clearly no heart. If he had truly loved her he would never have ruined her life that way. As long as she lived, she would never forgive him.

Tim's heart sank, seeing the blatant and bitter hatred transform her beautiful face. Until now his only question had been why? After she had built a solid life and career, why didn't she come back for him? And now he knew the answer. She didn't want to.

"So this is all his fault?"

Pashmina stared at him blankly.

"*You* were a married woman. *You* had an affair. But apparently it's his fault you got pregnant, and I paid the price."

Unconsciously she touched a hand to her cheek feeling the sting of his words as if he had slapped her. In a million years, he would never understand how much it cost her to give him up, her own flesh and blood, her own beautiful baby boy. As a woman without a country or a home she had nothing to give him but love, and that wasn't nearly enough. Her baby deserved a good life in a safe home with a loving family. And so she became a mother without a child.

"It was a mistake," she said so softly Tim had to lean in to hear her. "I'm sorry."

So was he. He couldn't remember a time he when he had felt worse than he did right now, and that was saying something. Dreaming of the day he would meet his parents was the only thing that had pulled him through the dark times, the loneliness, wondering what he had done wrong, wondering what was wrong with him. But this was way worse than that.

At least now Tim knew the truth. He gave Pashmina credit for that, for owning up to her mistake, for being straight with him. She had never wanted a baby; she had never wanted him. He was an accident she had walked away from.

Like mother like son. He stood, placing one sneakered foot slowly in front of the other as he headed to the door. Go. Don't look back. He wanted to run, afraid he might change his mind, but his resolve was stronger and the distance between them grew quickly.

"Tim, wait, where are you going?" Pashmina called, shocked and confused. "I'm not finished."

"Really?" he said, his voice flat and devoid of emotion. "I am."

CHAPTER FOURTEEN

After a morning spent waiting for Tim, praying he was all right, Amelia had finally given up and gone home. The day passed slowly, still without any word from him and her anxiety turned into anger. What a prick. This was low even for Tim.

Seeking refuge from her frustrated and restless mind, she took a cool, calming shower. This wasn't the first time he had left her hanging. Tim called it 'being independent.' *It's a dog eat dog world, Amelia, and the only one you can always count on is yourself.*

Bull shit. *What about the people you love, the people that love you?* She wanted to say, 'you can count on me,' but she didn't. She was too afraid. What if he didn't love her after all? She wasn't sure she could handle that. Sure he pissed her off sometimes, and maybe he'd hurt her a little, but he was good for her too. He made her feel cared for and safe and that couldn't be bad, could it?

Over breakfast, she and Ben had analyzed and dissected every facet of Tim's personality, formulating his pros and cons, alternately prosecuting and defending his character, playing judge and jury until neither one had anything more to say about him. In typical attorney fashion, Ben summed it up, "I guess he just is what he is."

Amelia started to protest, but Ben raised his hand. "I know that sounds trite, but it's true. We could spend all day trying to figure out what makes him tick but does it really matter? We both know he's never going to change."

Seeing the wheels turning in her head, he added, "And you can't change him either."

Sadly, Amelia nodded in resigned agreement. "So what do I do now?" she asked.

Rolling his coffee cup like a piece of clay between his hands, Ben avoided meeting her gaze. "Well, I guess that depends."

"On what?" she asked.

"On you," he sighed. "Do you want to accept him as he is, warts and all, or do you want to trust in yourself and maybe be better off without him?"

"When you put it that way, how I can lose?" she said dryly. "So those are my choices? Stay with the guy, never knowing where I stand or what to expect from him, or leave and prove he's right not to trust anybody but himself?"

Ben looked at her across the table. She looked so sad. *Damn you, Tim. Where are you?*

"I'm so sorry, Amelia. I wish things were different. I wish Tim was different. But he's got issues no one understands, not even me, and I've known him a long time. For some completely inexplicable reason, he's got some kind of built-in self-defense mechanism that works on reflex and keeps everyone at arm's length. Why? I don't know, but I know it's by choice and that he's created a protective bubble that he never leaves and that no one else can enter."

"What about love?" she asked in a pained whisper.

It was pointless to wait any longer. Reluctantly, Amelia had collected the few personal items she had started keeping in Tim's room back when she thought they had a future together, and left. Ben didn't try to stop her.

The ocean roared as Amelia's cell phone sang from the bathroom vanity where she had left it; buried in an array of brightly colored jars of moisturizers and tubes of mascara, lipsticks, blush, and eye shadows. Between her and Rose they could start a cosmetics store. In one fluid movement, she grabbed the phone and wrapped herself in a fluffy white bath sheet. *Please let this be Tim.* Sitting on the edge of her bed she answered tentatively. "Hello?"

"Hello, Amelia? I'm so sorry to bother you on a weekend, but I couldn't wait until Monday to speak with you."

Masking her disappointment, Amelia quickly assured Pashmina otherwise. "Gosh no, you could never be a bother. I'm really glad you called. I'm sorry I didn't have the guts to call you first."

Amelia's cheeks burned with embarrassment. "I really have to apologize for last night. I know it doesn't even begin to cover it, but please believe me when I say I am so, so sorry for everything: for running out on you, for Tim and how he treated you. I swear I don't know what got into him."

"You mean you haven't spoken to him?" Pashmina asked.

"Not yet," Amelia replied. "Last night I was livid and too pissed off to talk. And today I haven't been able to reach him at all."

At the other end of the phone Pashmina wondered what to do. Would it be better to share what she knew with Amelia little by little, like feeding bits of bread to a fragile bird, or tell her everything at once and trust that she could handle it?

"I think I might have an inkling…," Pashmina started.

"Well then, please share," said Amelia "because I sure as hell don't."

Pashmina hesitated. "Amelia, how long have you two been together?"

"Six months. Why?"

"Has Tim ever talked about his biological parents? Has he told you anything about them?"

Amelia hesitated, "Not much…a little bit recently." She waited for Pashmina to speak again. Did Pashmina know about George?

Pashmina closed her eyes. Clearly Amelia didn't know who Pashmina was, but maybe Tim had confided in her about George. It was a start at least. Already tired, Pashmina took a deep breath, filling her lungs to bursting and exhaling loudly. No time to waste, she better get started.

"Are you okay?" Amelia asked.

"I'm fine," Pashmina assured her. "Amelia, look, I have to tell you something but I'm not sure how. It was an incredible shock to me, and I'm pretty sure it will be to you, too."

Amelia stared longingly at the shower, where moments ago she had almost succeeded in washing her worries away. But that was then. Settling back against the bed pillows, she braced herself for whatever Pashmina was about to say, "Go ahead, I'm ready."

"Did Tim tell you about the surprise visit from his biological father a couple of weeks ago?"

Amelia was relieved. "I know all about it, they had a wonderful reunion." Feeling more confident she continued, "They even spent a few days together getting to know each other. Tim was ecstatic. He's been trying to find his parents forever, and when he learned that his dad had been looking for him, too, he was just beside himself."

"Well, that explains a lot. I think I understand why he was so upset with me last night."

Amelia stared quizzically at the phone, "You lost me."

"Remember the day we met, at lunch?" Pashmina asked. "Remember how you were a little intimidated by my reputation as a dragon lady, a diva?"

Amelia laughed. "I remember." It seemed like ages ago. "But I know better now, nothing could be further from the truth. You're a kind and wonderful woman."

"Thank you, but truthfully there's still a great deal you don't know about this Mistress of Mystery."

"Such as…?"

"Such as a long time ago I was married to the man of my dreams; he was perfect, except for his work. He traveled all the time," she explained. *Just stick to the facts, Pashmina, there's no excuse for what you did.* "I was very lonely and very weak and I had an affair. My husband found out and he left me. My lover deserted me, too, and then I discovered I was pregnant with his child."

Pashmina took a deep breath. It hurt going back in time. "I was distraught over losing my husband, and so ashamed of what I'd done, but more than anything I didn't want to hurt anyone else. So I left my home and my family and I came here, alone, where I could have the baby and arrange for it to be adopted without anyone knowing. I thought if I made everything normal again, then maybe Harry and I could get back together. That's what I hoped, but it didn't happen."

With no sound from Amelia, Pashsmina felt like she was talking to herself, a conversation long overdue but better late than never. She explained, "I was foolish and selfish and young but I thought I was doing the right thing for both of us. I didn't know the first thing about raising a baby. How would I support us? Where would we live?"

She heard the plea in her voice and thought of Tim. Was she too late? Would he ever forgive her? Pashmina continued, resolute, "I was convinced I knew nothing about being a mother, until now. When Tim came to see me this morning he made me realize that there's no substitute for a mother's love; it's the only thing a child really needs."

"This morning?"

Amelia's first words after Pashmina's lengthy monologue startled them both, but thank God, at least she didn't feel so alone anymore. Pashmina apologized, "I'm afraid he stood you up for me. He wanted to talk about the fireworks at dinner last night, but he got so angry and upset again that he left before I could explain anything to him. I'm afraid he's inherited his father's quick temper and rash behavior."

"I don't understand." Amelia's head was buzzing, trying to make sense of what Pashmina was saying.

"Amelia, this is what I wanted to tell you." She swallowed, "Tim is my son. He's the baby I gave away. I am his mother." Pasmina began to cry.

"I don't understand," Amelia said again, massaging her suddenly throbbing forehead. "If you're his mother, why would Tim be such a jerk to you? I just told you that nothing is more important to him than knowing who his parents are."

Reaching for a nearby box of tissues, Pashmina dried her tears. "Except having your parents want to find you, maybe?"

"What do you mean?"

She explained, "When you joined us for dinner, Tim already knew the truth about me. George told him. But he didn't say anything. I don't know why, maybe he was too nervous, and then my comments about adoption must have struck a nerve. So he left without saying anything. This morning, he must have thought twice about it, and he came to see me, to tell me."

"I don't believe you," said Amelia, her pleasant voice suddenly harsh.

"You think I'm lying?" Pashmina was taken aback. Of all the possible ways Amelia might have reacted, Pashmina hadn't considered this. From the moment they met, she had felt a connection to the young woman, an unexpected kinship and warmth, and an overwhelming need to protect her. Now she felt the painful sting of her accusation.

"Amelia, I'd never do that. I'd never lie to you," Pashmina promised.

Amelia didn't know what to do. Find Tim and make him explain everything, or keep listening to Pashmina's crazy but not implausible stories. A chilling thought washed over her; one of them was lying, but which one?

"If you're telling the truth," Amelia said, releasing the words slowly one by one, "that would mean Tim has been lying to me. He told me about George, about meeting his dad, nothing about you."

"I'm not lying." Pashmina said firmly.

That meant it was Tim, but why would he lie to her? So they weren't perfect, but what couple was? On any given day, one person always gave more than the other, and it all balanced out in the end. Usually. She had been carrying the ball for so long now, it felt like she didn't even have a partner anymore.

"You have to be," Amelia begged. "Please."

Hearing her tearful plea, Pashmina's heart broke. "I'm sorry, I wish I was. That would be easier than hurting you like this."

"But why…?" Amelia's voice cracked, but the question was clear.

"I blame myself," Pashmina said. "If I'd acted differently, made the right choice all those years ago, maybe Tim would be a different person, too."

"Spoken like a true mother," Amelia sniffed, using the backs of her hands to wipe away her tears.

Pashmina smiled for the first time in what felt like forever. "Thank you, I'll take that as a compliment. I'm just sorry it took me this long to start acting like one."

"I still can't believe he'd keep something this big, this important from me, it's as bad as lying in my book. What does it say about our relationship?"

Pashmina shook her head. "Only Tim can answer that, I'm afraid. And he has a lot more explaining to do, too. I told him everything, every last dirty, shameful detail about my life and he shared nothing of his. No more throwing stones at glass houses. It's his turn to talk now."

"Amen to that," Amelia prayed. "So how do we make that happen?"

"Well, he's made it pretty clear he doesn't want to see or speak to me again, so for now at least I need to give him some space." Tapping her fingernails rhythmically on the cherry end table beside her, Pashmina considered their options. "But there is something I can do. I'll need your help, Amelia. I hope you're okay with that."

"Absolutely."

"Perfect. Can you come see me tomorrow? I need to talk to you about the book."

Surprised, Amelia asked, "What's the book got to do with anything?"

The unmistakable sound of a dial tone signaled in her ear and Amelia shrugged. The conversation was over, for now at least. It had been a long, drama-filled day and she was one hundred percent drained.

With a yawning stretch, she settled back against the pillows, her mind weary but still busy with thoughts of Tim, Pashmina, and George. Theirs was a complicated triangle for sure, but what bearing could it possibly have on Pashmina's book?

She twitched suddenly, her reflexes startling, as Pashmina's face came into focus behind Amelia's sleep-heavy eyes.

"Everything," said the author fervently. "Everything."

CHAPTER FIFTEEN

Tim walked purposefully with long, even strides that quickly brought him to Caesar's. Waving off the excessively cheerful hostess, he headed straight to the bar for a drink. "Hey, Brett."

Glancing up from washing glasses at the sink, the short, muscular bartender walked over to Tim, grateful for the reprieve from his mundane duties. "Hey, Tim," he greeted his regular customer with a friendly handshake and cheerful smile. "Where've you been?" He placed a cocktail napkin and a small bowl of peanuts in front of him. "I haven't seen you in a while."

"Yeah, I've been busy." Tim grabbed the napkin mindlessly, folding the edges. "It's been a hell of a few weeks."

"Sorry to hear that, man." Like most bartenders, Brett was both a drink server and a confessor for his patrons when they needed to get things off their chests, which was most of the time. "So what can I get you to ease the pain?" He smiled sympathetically.

"Give me a Stella and a shot of tequila and keep them coming." Brett frowned, and Tim assured him, "Don't worry, I walked here. Just keep them coming and there's a big mother fucking tip coming your way."

With a nod, Brett went in search of beer and tequila wondering just what kind of hellish happenings called for the alcoholic power of two to set things right. Tim was a conservative drinker. He never lost control and never let his guard down, but this deadly duo was going to set him on his ass in no time. Brett grabbed a beer, poured a generous shot of tequila, and placed them both in front of an expectant Tim.

"Bottoms up!" Raising the shot glass in silent salute, Tim tipped it quickly down his throat.

The Red Sox game was on TV and Tim watched it, sipping on his beer. Things must really be bad if he was watching baseball, but it was better than the alternative. Thinking about Pashmina was painful, thinking about Amelia was complicated. Better just to drink, watch baseball, and not think at all.

* * *

"Jesus, Tim, where've you been? I've been looking for you everywhere."

The familiar voice seeped into Tim's drunken consciousness, many hours and several rounds later. He turned slowly, allowing his vision to steady until he saw only one Ben. "Hey, man. Let me buy you a drink."

Taking a seat next to him, Ben regarded his friend with a critical eye. "How many have you already put away?"

"Who's counting? Brett!" Waving a hand at the bartender Tim motioned for two more. "This round's on me," he slurred as Brett set two beers in front of them. "To Ben, you're a good man," Tim toasted, clinking his bottle with Ben's. "So tell me what's it like, Golden Boy?"

"What what's like?"

"What's it like to shit gold, to have *eeeveryone* love you?"

Ben chuckled. "I wish I knew." He glanced at Tim's humorless face and sobered immediately. "What's this all about? What're you doing here alone, bombed out of your mind?"

Sprawled across the bar now, his head resting heavily on one arm, Tim was barely lucid. "I resemble that remark," he declared struggling to lift the concrete weight that was his head.

"I'm serious, Tim. What's going on with you? You're picking fights with famous people, avoiding your girlfriend and ditching me. You're not always the easiest guy to be around, but you're better than that. It's not you."

"What makes you so sure?" Ben moved closer, struggling to hear Tim better. "Maybe it's in my genes."

What? Taking a stab in the dark Ben asked, "Does this have anything to do with George?"

"Ding, ding, ding, ding," Tim tapped his finger to his nose signaling a winner. "Very good, Golden Boy, but don't forget we all have a daddy *and* a mommy. Do you know who my mommy is?"

In another minute Tim was going to fall off the bar stool. "Okay, Big Guy, I think you've had enough. Let's get you home." Pulling some money from his wallet, Ben paid the bill.

"No! You haven't answered my question yet." Tim was insistent. "Do you know who my mommy is?"

"Mrs. Smith. She's your mother."

"Buzzzz, wrong answer. My mother is the beautiful and talented Pashmina Papadakis."

"Yeah right, c'mon, let's go," Ben said, attempting to pull Tim off the stool. Tim waved his hands wildly, trying to slap Ben away.

"No, seriously, Pashmina's my real mother," he enunciated the syllables, "my bio-logi-cal mother." Ignoring Ben's dubious look, he rambled on, "Yep, I know you don't believe me, but it's true. George told me so and then Pashmina told me. But she doesn't want me. Nobody wants me."

Hunched over the bar like a deflated balloon, Tim babbled softly to himself while Ben tried to sort it all out. Some things did kind of make sense now, like why Tim had hightailed it out of their apartment this morning, and why he had left him to calm Amelia. One more thing Tim had kept from her.

Honestly, if Ben lived to be a hundred, he would never understand Tim's obsessive privacy and secretive ways.

Tim's drunken voice assaulted his ears, singing of loneliness and depression.

"Where are you coming up with this bullshit? Not only do you have your adoptive family, but now you've got your birthparents, too."

"Birth father," Tim corrected. "I'm serious. Pashmina doesn't want me."

Ben was more than skeptical. "She said that?"

"Not in so many words, but I could tell."

"You could tell. And I suppose you can just tell your parents don't want you either. Because they couldn't make it to Parents' Weekends or graduation? They explained all that to you—your dad had business out of the country and your mom went with him. But we had some good times with my family, right?"

"Sure."

Ben felt bad for him. "Look, they may not have always been there when you wanted them to be, but I know your parents love you."

"You don't know Jack shit." Tim's drunken haze was dissipating.

Ben countered quickly, "I know you wish your parents were around more, that they were more involved, and I'm sure they did the best they could. If you asked them..."

"Can't do that." Tim cut Ben off mid-sentence. "Wanna know why?" Leaning close to Ben, he whispered loud enough for everyone to hear, "Because they don't exist. Ha!"

Expecting shock or disbelief, Tim peered at Ben, and saw disappointment written all over his face. "I don't know what kind of a bullshit story you're telling, but you need to stop. Now."

"I'm not bullshitting you, it's true. There were never any parents. I made them up. I made all of it up."

"What do you mean you have no parents? Everybody has parents."

Drunk and tired, Tim was quiet, but Ben wasn't about to let him clam up now. Whether he liked it or not, he was going to talk until Ben had all the answers he needed. Signaling Brett, Ben ordered water and coffee for both of them. They were going to be here a while.

"Okay, buddy, start talking. I don't care if you slur every last goddamned word. If you're telling me that you made everything up, I sure as hell want to know why."

Tim nodded, relieved. He had been stoic for so long, keeping up the charade. It was exhausting and he didn't want to do it anymore. He was just going to let it all out and let whatever happened happen.

"Well, to use an old expression, I was born out of wedlock and my mother, Pashmina, gave me up for adoption. Until a few weeks ago when George told me, I never knew who my birth mother was or the circumstances of my birth. In a nutshell, I was never adopted. I lived in an orphanage and then a group home until I was eighteen and earned a scholarship to college. I've been on my own ever since."

Tim had never seen Ben at a loss for words before. "I lived in a few foster homes, but no one ever wanted me permanently, they always sent me back to the orphanage until another foster home became available." In and out, in and out, Tim had gone to every new home full of hope that this time it would stick, that this time he would find his family. By the time he was eight, his faith was shattered. He became a juvenile delinquent, raising hell, getting into trouble, rejecting anyone who might have helped before they could reject him.

"College was my reward for eighteen years of solitary confinement. After all that time alone in a system that couldn't have cared less about me, I was finally on my own with the power to do what I wanted, to make my own decisions."

"So there you have it. Story time's over," Tim announced, sliding off the stool, holding onto the bar for support. "I've gotta take a leak."

Ben stood in stunned silence and concurred, they could both use a break. "Let's go home. We'll talk more in the morning."

CHAPTER SIXTEEN

Bright sun streamed through the window creating a symphony of light that set the dust motes dancing and tickling Amelia's nose until she sneezed fully awake and alert. It was seven o'clock. Shaking off the remains of sleep, she savored the early morning quiet of her room, her mind blissfully blank and carefree.

To her surprise, she had actually slept through the night peacefully, without any wild and crazy dreams disturbing her unconscious state. And now she felt good, ready to seize the day despite the chaos it promised to bring. In a little while, she would have to deal with the turmoil of Tim and Pashmina, but right now her stomach was rumbling, an angry and hungry reminder of how long it had been since she had last eaten. Tim and Pashmina could wait, breakfast was her first priority.

Rose stared unabashedly as Amelia entered the kitchen, taking critical note of her fluffy pink robe and matching fuzzy slippers. "Well, good morning, Sleeping Beauty," she drawled, pointing to the open gossip rag in front of her. "News flash, the Easter Bunny wants his suit back."

"Very funny." Amelia grabbed the tabloid away from her. "*Famous & Fabulous*, Rose? Seriously, is this where you're getting your information these days?"

Rose lunged for the magazine as Amelia spun out of reach, calling out articles in her best entertainment reporter's voice, " 'Which Celi-butts have Cellulite?', 'The Real Truth About Reality TV'. Oh, hold on, this one's my favorite and a must-read for all you struggling actors out there, 'Casting Couch Crud: Be Careful Where You Sit!'"

Tears of laughter streamed from Amelia's eyes. "Is this why you're up with the birds this morning?"

"Early to bed, early to rise." Rose's pretty pink lips pursed together in a petulant pout.

"Go ahead, don't believe me," she dared, challenging the blatant doubt on her friend's face. "Truth is I had no one to go out with last night; you were comatose and nobody else was around. What choice did I have?" She shrugged disconsolately, "What a waste of a Saturday night."

"A good night's sleep is hardly tragic," Amelia reminded her, laughing at Rose's mournful expression. "Think of it as beauty rest," she consoled. "And I must say, you do look wonderful."

Beaming, Rose gave her a quick hug and handed her a Diet Coke. "Thanks, you look great, too. So what's on the agenda today? Want to have a girls' day out or are you doing something with Timmy Poo?"

"Neither, I'm afraid. I'm going to Pashmina's."

"On Sunday, what for?" Filling her cup with equal parts coffee, cream, and sugar, Rose sipped and sighed contentedly.

"I'm not really sure," Amelia mused, unable to keep anything from Rose. "All I know is that Pashmina is Tim's mother, he's upset with her and won't talk to me, and somehow this is all connected to Pashmina's book."

"Sorry," Rose said, wiggling a delicate pinky in one ear. "I thought you said Pashmina is Tim's mother?"

"You heard right." Grabbing cold pizza from the refrigerator, Amelia took another swig of her soda and tore off a chunk of pepperoni topping. Delicious.

"Can you believe it?" Amelia continued talking between ravenous bites. "Pashmina is Tim's mother. Now I know what they mean when they say the truth is stranger than fiction."

"I guess so." Preoccupied with her own breakfast preparations, Rose was momentarily distracted. She slathered a thick layer of whipped cream cheese over her Asiago bagel, topped off her cup of cream and sugar with a little more coffee, and turned back to Amelia. "How'd you find out?"

"Not from Tim, that's for sure. Pashmina called and told me."

Amelia ran a frustrated hand through her hair. "When I think about what he put me through Friday night, I could kill him. It was the most humiliating moment of my life, or it was until yesterday at least. Do you have any idea how embarrassing it is to admit that your boyfriend doesn't trust you enough to confide in you? Maybe it's a sign I should just cut him loose."

"Whoa, Sea Biscuit, don't jump to any conclusions before you have all the facts." Impersonating the voice of reason, Rose surprised them both. "What did Tim say?"

"Nothing, that's the problem. He's avoiding me."

"Are you sure?" Maybe Amelia was just being melodramatic.

Finger by finger Amelia began ticking off her reasons. "I haven't spoken to him since he drove me home from dinner. He hasn't called or returned my calls. He purposely left his apartment when I told him I was coming over to talk. He never said a word to me about Pashmina, even though he's known about her for weeks. He didn't even tell me he'd met his biological father until after he'd left town. What would you think?" she finished bitterly.

"I'd think he was avoiding me," Rose agreed. Not for the first time, she wished she had never let Amelia go out with him in the first place. "So what now?"

"I don't know. I guess I'll see what Pashmina's thinking first then figure out my own plan for dealing with Tim. If I ever find him," she added.

Rose toasted in solemn agreement. She hated to say 'I told you so,' but she had always thought Amelia was too good for Tim.

As Amelia foraged for more pizza, Rose flipped quickly through the pages of *Famous & Fabulous* in search of divine guidance for her friend. But besides a debate on whether or not Rihanna should take Chris Brown back, the skinny on Kirstie's umpteenth incredible weight loss, and a pregnant actress guessing game of 'is she or isn't she?', the gossip oracle lacked any insight to real people problems like Amelia's. Disappointed, Rose closed the magazine, wishing she could be a better friend and help Amelia figure things out; but just like *Famous & Fabulous*, Rose didn't have any answers either.

* * *

Eager to hear what Pashmina was planning, Amelia rushed to her home, never slowing until the author's Beacon Hill townhouse came into view. But as Amelia approached the quaint brick building with its tendrils of ivy climbing gracefully up the front walls, a sudden fit of nerves threatened to overwhelm her. This was one of those life-altering moments when for better or worse a simple act can set the wheels of your future into dizzying, out of control motion. In the movies, it's the part where audiences squirm in their seats, silently urging the onscreen character forward into the unknown or screaming them back to safety. Which would it be for her?

Before she could knock or change her mind and run away, the door opened and Pashmina pulled Amelia inside like she was saving her from an oncoming train. "I'm so glad you're here, we have a lot to do today," she said. "Would you like something to drink, coffee, soda, water?"

Clasping Amelia's hand firmly in her own, Pashmina led her into the study where just 24 hours before she and Tim had sat. But today would be different. Today she and Amelia would actually start to make things right between Pashmina and her son, and if they were really lucky, maybe they could patch things up between Amelia and Tim too.

"All set for the moment, thanks." Sheepishly Amelia raised her hand. She was holding a Diet Coke. "I brought my own."

"I'm good, too, so maybe we should just get started then."

"Sure, but I don't really know what that means," Amelia confessed. "Do you want to talk about the book or Tim?"

Still holding Amelia's hand, Pashmina guided her to a seat on the couch and contemplated her answer. Amelia was waiting patiently for Pashmina to speak, so different from Tim, though in his defense he had wanted more than just information. For the thousandth time that day, Pashmina wished he hadn't left before she could explain herself.

Choosing her words carefully, Pashmina began, "In my mind, they're not mutually exclusive. Although I had a hand in creating both of them, only one is truly mine." Amelia's head tilted to one side, confused. "Tim is my son." Pashmina sighed. "He might not like it very much, but that's the undeniable truth. On the other hand, *Family Secrets* is not my story; it belongs to someone else, someone who hurt me deeply, and who I wanted to hurt back."

She paused, organizing her thoughts. "I thought if I shared this person's story with the world, I could expose him and ruin his life like he ruined mine."

Tears glistened in Pashmina's eyes as Amelia tried to understand what she was saying. Her lips were moving but she wasn't making any sense. Not knowing what to say, Amelia stayed quiet, patting Pashmina's hand comfortingly.

"But I can't do it," Pashmina gulped, openly crying now. "I won't do it...for Tim's sake. For years I didn't do anything, but not anymore. I won't hurt him again."

Her chin lifted slightly as quiet determination settled over her. "I'm pulling *Family Secrets.*"

Amelia didn't react right away. A movie reel of memories flashed through her head. Wasn't it just yesterday she was profusely thanking Stuart for making her editor of Pashmina Papadakis' new novel, pumping his hand enthusiastically and fighting the impulse to hug him? She couldn't believe it. It didn't take a genius to know what a plum assignment this was. More than that, it was the apex of professional success, something she hadn't even realized was important to her until now.

Her mother always said 'anything less than well done is half-baked' so though she had never considered herself an overachiever, Amelia always tried her best at everything she did. She was good at her job, she knew it; and with this career boost Stuart was showing her that he knew it too. If Pashmina pulled the book, it could be the end of Amelia's brief and shining career. Over her dead body.

Focusing on the woman in question, Amelia tried to stay calm, "Let's just slow down a minute. Are you telling me that publishing *Family Secrets* could hurt Tim?"

"Yes."

"Okaay," Amelia let the word hang between them. She needed more than that to work with. "Would you mind telling me how?"

"It isn't my story." Pashmina cut to the chase, "It was a rough manuscript I've had in my possession for years. I simply refined it to be more in line with my other novels."

"I see." Amelia had a sinking feeling she had just hit a Titanic-size iceberg. "So the book isn't yours, or at very least credit for it belongs to someone else. Have I got that right?"

Pashmina blushed slightly, but answered, "That's right. None of it, the idea, the plot, not even the title is mine."

Stunned, Amelia looked at Pashmina, so beautiful and composed. Author extraordinaire or plagiarizing fake? Will the real Pashmina please stand up? "I don't know what to say, this is just incredible." *Incredibly bad.* With a forced confidence Amelia didn't feel, she added, "Fortunately, you've got an incredible editor. Don't worry, I'll find a way around this."

"No!" Pashmina raised a panicked hand. "You don't understand. I don't want to find a way around it. I want to throw it away and forget all about it."

"What?" Amelia panicked too. "You can't do that!"

Besides a binding contract, Pashmina was overlooking her promise to all the loyal fans eagerly awaiting her next great read. "Pashmina you *have* to release a book this year." She squeezed Pashmina's hands tightly. "Please, tell me what's going on. Tell me and I promise I'll do everything I can to help."

Their eyes locked in a contest of wills, blue versus brown, but Amelia refused to budge. No one was going anywhere until she knew the truth, no matter how awful that truth might be.

Pashmina caved first. Everything would be fine if she trusted Amelia, she had to believe that. "The manuscript is George's," she confessed, relaxing a little as the burdensome secret poured from her lips. "He wrote it, he lived it, and he gave it to me for safekeeping just before he disappeared." Sharing was easier than she had thought it would be. Feeling better by the minute, she continued.

"To tell you the truth, I'd forgotten all about it until a year or so ago. I was home visiting my family and I ran into George." She remembered the shock of seeing him again, he looking older but handsome as ever. He had studied her with a possessive arrogance that was annoying and flattering at the same time. "We hadn't seen each other in almost thirty years. Needless to say, we had a lot of catching up to do," she smiled wryly.

"George told me everything that had happened to him, why he left so suddenly, why he didn't tell me he was going, so many things I never knew about and by the time he finished talking I wanted to kill him as much as the Greek mob did." Bitterness stung her throat; George had overstepped his bounds without an ounce of concern for her or what she wanted. Was a lifetime of happiness with Harry too much to ask?

"I gave up my own child for a second chance with Harry. I'm not proud of that, and I regret my decision every day, but what George did was worse; he stole my life, he made sure I'd never have the future I hoped for." She begged Amelia to understand, "I couldn't let him get away with it, taking everything from me like that, so I decided to publish his story knowing full-well he still has enemies who want to harm him, knowing exactly how it would turn his world upside down."

"But that's all changed," Pashmina said, coming back into the present. "Now that Tim's in the picture, I've changed my mind. For better or worse, Tim knows who his father is now. If I hurt George, I'll hurt Tim too, and probably lose him forever. I'm not willing to take that chance."

Drained and dying of thirst, Pashmina stood to get some water. Amelia quenched her thirst, too, polishing off the remains of her soda in one long gulp. What she really needed was a shot of something stronger, something to slow the spinning in her head and help her process what had just happened.

Pashmina handed her a glass of water. "This is all way more complicated than I realized," Amelia proclaimed between non-alcoholic sips. *Duh.* She bit her lip trying to think of something else to say, something ingenious, something that wouldn't have Pashmina doubting her mental aptitude. "But it could be worse, you know?" *Oh yeah, that was much better. Solid.*

"It is a predicament," Pashmina agreed. "But I've made up my mind. *Family Secrets* can't be published." She felt terrible. After all, it was her fault they were in this jam, but it wouldn't be the first time an editor had to clean up after an author either. It was time to see what Amelia was really made of.

Amelia was nauseous. How did this happen? Her world was imploding in epic proportions and she didn't have a clue what to do about it. She thought about her mother, and for the first time in a long time wished she was here. From the day she was born, it seemed Amelia had been locked in battle with Francesca, arguing constantly over everything from hemlines and hairstyles to college and career choices. Francesca had an opinion about everything, and pity the fool who didn't share her thinking. She was hard-headed and strong-willed, a one-two punch combination that infuriated Amelia even as she secretly admired her mother's seemingly infinite strength, a resilient force that had carried them both through some difficult times.

When Amelia was five years old, her dad had suffered a heart attack. She had woken up one night to the sound of crushing stones and an ambulance speeding up their white pebbled driveway. From her bedroom window she had watched as the EMT's wheeled her dad from the house, a plastic oxygen mask covering his face. Weak though he was, he had waved to her, barely managing to move his hand back and forth, and she had waved back uncomprehending.

"Amelia, go back to bed," her mother called from beside the ambulance. She had looked sad, sadder than Amelia had ever seen her, resigned to the fact she was losing her husband. But to her daughter, she seemed like an Amazon, tall, strong, and invincible. A widow at thirty-five, Francesca never remarried, but dedicated herself to Amelia, acting as both mother and father, struggling to find the balance between the two and not always succeeding.

Francesca was a tough taskmaster, and though Amelia understood why, it didn't make it any easier to swallow. She had spent her youth challenging her mother at every turn, pushing every single one of her buttons whenever she had the chance. But no matter how bad it got, how long they went without speaking, Amelia always knew her mother loved her, and like it or not, her mother was usually right about most things. So what would Francesca say now, what would she do if she was in Amelia's shoes?

Channeling her inner Francesca, Amelia called on her mother's practical sense of logic and cool objectivity. There had to be something she could do to make things right. *Ignore the hype, pinpoint the problem, and focus on the facts.* She could almost feel Francesca beside her. Okay, so the problem is that Pashmina is refusing to release her book and both of our careers are headed down the drain. *Forget the hype and stick to the facts.*

Fact, Pashmina is Tim's mother. Fact, George is Tim's father. Fact, Pashmina loves Tim and hates George. Fact, George wrote a self-incriminating manuscript and Pashmina has it. Fact, Pashmina intends to break George and destroy him with his own manuscript. Fact, if she hurts George she hurts Tim too. Fact, she won't hurt Tim, she loves him. Fact, Amelia's screwed.

Stop personalizing. Tell me about the book, is it good? Really good, Amelia thought, but different, not Pashmina's usual style. *Well obviously, she didn't write it.* Yes and no, she actually re-worked the book extensively in places to make it more hers. *So would you say she co-wrote the book?*

Amelia had to think about that for a minute. Technically George and Pashmina had both contributed to the story, but could you call them co-authors if one didn't know about the other? Not that it mattered. They weren't even speaking to each other much less working together. No, it was pretty safe to say that Tim would be their one and only collaboration.

Ok, what else? Amelia scowled. If I knew what else would I be sitting here having an imaginary conversation with my mother? *Testy, testy, but remember, dear, your mother is always right.* I know, I know. I'm trying but I just can't figure it out. *Can't or won't? The Amelia I raised never took 'no' for an answer.*

Well, that was true. Amelia almost laughed remembering all the times she faced off against her mother. It was nice to be on the same side for a change. "That's it!" she squeaked, startling Pashmina out of her own thoughts.

"What, what's 'it'?"

"We're going about this all wrong. We're acting like this is a war we have to win." Amelia spoke firmly, "I'm telling you right now, Pashmina, if we fight this, we'll lose everything."

Pashmina's stomach knotted. "So what do you suggest we do?" she asked.

"Play nice," Amelia said, ignoring Pashmina's dubious stare. Amelia didn't care, for the first time in a long time, she felt good, better yet, she felt confident. It took a while to put all the pieces of the puzzle together, but she had finally done it and now she understood exactly what she had to do. "We need to work together, as a team. Do you understand what I'm saying? "

Pashmina waved her hand dismissively, "Not at all. What the heck are you talking about?"

"I'm talking about getting your book published with your reputation intact, and a second chance at a fresh start with your son. Isn't that what you want?" Pashmina nodded. "Then hear me out." Feeling like General Patton, Amelia began to pace, her hands clasped behind her, explaining as she went.

"Right now you and I are the only two people who know the truth behind *Family Secrets*. Pashmina started to object, but Amelia forged on. "Of course George knows it too, but he doesn't know that you're planning to tell his story to the world. And Tim knows nothing about any of this, but when he finds out, he'll be devastated. What we need to do is publish the book without endangering George and enlightening Tim." She glanced at Pashmina who was still looking at her, skeptically.

"I know, I know," Amelia said, raising her hands in mock surrender, "it seems like a mission impossible, but maybe not. What if you were to change the book's most incriminating details like names and places to protect George's identity? It's still a great story, but no harm's done to George."

Pashmina was quiet. "What if George told Tim about his past?" she asked at last. "He'll know the book is about his father even if it doesn't name him, and he'll hold it against me."

Amelia knelt in front of Pashmina, ready to share the final details of her plan. "But what if it's not your book?" she asked. "What if someone else wrote it?"

Incredulous, Pashmina looked at her. "Who else could have written it?"

Ignoring the question, Amelia asked, "Have you ever heard of a book called *Primary Colors*? It's a fictional novel based upon the real life characters and events making up the political scene of the 1990s. Long story short, it's the most talked about political novel ever, three million copies sold and nearly one million dollars in sales generated in the first year alone and do you know why?" Excited, Amelia didn't wait for Pashmina to respond. "Because *Primary Colors* was put out by an anonymous author, a fact that many people credit for the book's incredible success. Curiosity about a book written by Anonymous produced more publicity and generated more sales without anyone even questioning the author's personal knowledge or involvement."

"That's your plan?" Pashmina was coming out of her stupor. "You want to release *Family Secrets* from an anonymous author?"

"Exactly!" Amelia began pacing again. "We publish *Family Secrets* as a novel written by an anonymous author. Of course we at Dewes know that it's your work so the terms of your contract are met in full AND quite possibly this will generate book sales that exceed projected numbers. George's identity is protected, and he'll never argue the use of his manuscript since that would only bring unwanted attention on him and his past indiscretions. And Tim will know beyond a doubt the lengths you went to to ensure that no one was hurt by your professional obligations. It's a win-win-win-win situation!"

Time stood still as Pashmina considered her options. This was it. This was the way out for all of them. Amelia felt like she had just ascended the summit of Mt. Everest. Suddenly everything was so clear, so obvious. Her plan could work, but only if she had Pashmina's support, too. From the corner of her eye she could see Pashmina sitting on the couch, hands clasped, head bowed. It was impossible to tell what she was thinking.

Was this madness or genius, Pashmina wondered? More importantly, would it work? So many questions, so many unknowns it made her nervous, downright scared in fact, but what choice did she have? She could break her contract and suffer a professional tar and feathering and still be without her son, or she could join Amelia's 'team' and maybe win big all around, big emphasis on maybe. So who was the crazy one now, Amelia with her swing-on-a-star optimism, or Pashmina saddling up for the ride?

Amelia turned nervously as Pashmina approached, hand extended. "Hello," she said, her voice strong and clear, "Allow me to introduce myself. My name is Anonymous."

CHAPTER SEVENTEEN

Surrounded by darkness, Pashmina lay in bed taking no comfort from the soft caress of the silky sheets or the weighted warmth of the duvet covering her protectively. The eerie glow emanating from the digital alarm clock beside her was mesmerizing. She watched the minutes tick by, one hundred and eighty minutes to be exact, since she had first laid her head on the pillow, no closer to sleep now than she had been three hours ago. She was beyond exhausted.

What a difference a few hours can make. Earlier, waving an excited Amelia off to her office, eager to get their crazy plan underway, Pashmina had felt almost euphoric. This was going to work, and when it did, she would be the happiest woman on Earth. And the luckiest, thanks to Amelia. The young editor had really gone above and beyond this time.

Then Pashmina thought of Tim, and was gripped by a sudden rush of love. She had seen her son only three times in twenty-nine years, but it was the first time Pashmina treasured the most.

It had been dark and rainy when the taxi pulled up in front of the Horizon House of Hope for Mothers and Their Babies. Reluctant to leave the comfortable warmth of the cab, Pashmina peered out the window to examine her temporary new home. Our home she thought unconsciously, rubbing her rounded belly and eliciting a resounding kick in response. She smiled; they were quite the pair.

Pashmina paid the driver, and made a mad dash for the door as the rain pelted down, cold and wet. Wrapping her coat securely around her precious cargo, she bent low, determined to protect her child as best she could in the time they had left together. It wouldn't be long. She could already feel the heaviness moving down her body as the baby made ready for its arrival. Soon she would give birth to a baby boy or girl, her constant companion all this time, and she was terrified.

What if she couldn't go through with it? When the nurse came to take her baby from her, what if she wouldn't let go? She knew it was the right thing to do. Her baby deserved a good home and a family that would give it all the things she couldn't, but her heart broke just thinking about it. They belonged together.

It was true. Somewhere along the way Pashmina had fallen in love with her unborn child, and now her love would be tested in the worst way possible. She needed to be strong, strong enough to let her baby go.

When her water inevitably broke, Pashmina cried. This was it. The fierce cries of her newborn child filled the room as the doctor handed the baby to her, "This little one refuses to be ignored." Extending her arms she welcomed the baby into her embrace. It was a boy, beautiful and healthy with ten fingers, ten toes, a shock of thick hair and almond-shaped eyes just like hers. He was perfect. Her heart broke.

"I'm sorry, dear, but it's time to say good-bye."

She looked at the nurse with tear-filled eyes, her arms trembling as she gave the child to her like a precious gift. "Wait," Pashmina called before the woman could leave the room. "I almost forgot." She reached around her neck, unclasping the only thing of value she had left. Her mother had given it to her, the gold medallion of St. Barbara, the patron saint of protection. The medallion was still warm with the heat of her body as she placed it carefully over the baby's head. "Be safe, Little One, be strong," she whispered, her voice cracking as a fresh wave of tears overtook her. If she was doing the right thing, why did it feel so horribly wrong?

"Please go," she begged the nurse, "before I change my mind."

Nodding sympathetically, the nurse left the room without another word.

* * *

Tears trickled down Pashmina's cheeks, leaving a maze of salty tracks in their wake. Rubbing her hands across her face, she grabbed a robe from the end of the bed and stumbled through the darkness, her mind too busy for sleep, too tired to bother with lights, and headed for the oasis of her moonlit kitchen.

Bathed in blue-white beams, Pashmina warmed a pot of milk on the stove, watching with fascination as chocolate shavings swirled and danced, blending delicately into the foamy white liquid. With a cup in hand, she made her way to the parlor, a small hexagonal room, filled with an eclectic collection of personal memorabilia and treasured memories. This was her private sanctuary, the place she came to escape and get away from it all.

But tonight she was here for a different reason; she was going to set things right the only way she knew how. An elegant writing table stood sentry in a corner of the room, a petite desk lamp perched on top illuminating the intimate space and revealing a small cache of pens and personal stationary. She sat, placing a crisp piece paper neatly in front of her, and grasping one of the smooth, cold pens between her fingers, she began to write.

The words came slowly at first as she struggled to organize the onslaught of memories that threatened to overwhelm her; she had a lot of explaining to do. Though Tim had made it perfectly clear he wasn't interested in anything she had to say, she hoped and prayed he would give her another chance. With increasing urgency, she steered her pen rapidly across the page, the words tumbling down like rain drops. She would write until she couldn't, until there was nothing more to say, and then she would personally see that it reached Tim's hands. Nothing was going to stop her this time.

At Tim and Ben's apartment, the morning sunshine assaulted Ben's face and demanded that he open his eyes. Reluctantly, he complied, instantly jumpstarting his sleepy brain into a buzz of cerebral activity. Last night at Caesar's seemed so surreal that he still couldn't get his head around it. Clearly, their conversation was far from over but getting Tim home before he crashed and burned had taken everything Ben had. Emotionally spent and physically worn out, Ben had called it a night too.

Pushing off the bedcovers, he padded barefoot to the kitchen to start a pot of coffee. It was a high-test kind of morning for sure. Pouring two mugs, he headed for Tim's room, edging the door open with his foot, and peered inside. The room was dark, the shades were drawn, and Tim was still asleep under a pile of sheets and blankets. The bedside clock read 11:00 A.M., a respectable hour for rising.

Ben placed the mugs on top of a dresser and approached the side of the bed, ready to rouse the sleeping dead with a gentle nudge. "Hey, Tim. Tim." No response. He nudged harder. "Time to wake up and face the day, buddy." Not so much as a muscle twitched; maybe Tim really was dead. Concerned, Ben bent to check Tim's breathing, and was trapped by the glare of one blood-shot eye.

"What the fuck do you think you're doing?"

"Making sure you're still alive."

Tim's head felt like a giant battering ram. "Shit, I wish I wasn't."

"Thought you might feel that way. I brought you some coffee." Extending the steaming cup in front of him, Ben waited patiently for Tim to claim it.

"Sometimes you are a godsend," Tim croaked between grateful sips.

"You're welcome." The caffeine was doing its job and being the supreme friend that Ben was, it was time for him to do his. "Tim, we've got to talk about last night."

Tim didn't move, and Ben wondered if he had even heard him. "What's there to talk about?" Tim finally replied.

"Well, for one thing, I want to thank you for telling me everything. It's un-fucking-believable what you've gone through. I know it took a lot for you to tell me." He perched carefully on the side of the bed, worried what he said next would get him kicked to the hardwood floor.

"For another thing, I think you've got some more explaining to do, to Pashmina and to Amelia." Tim's head shot up like a cork. "They both deserve to know the truth too."

"I bet Pashmina doesn't have a clue where your head's at right now. Did you even say anything to her or did you just walk out in typical Tim fashion?" Tim's head dropped. Ben had called that one right. "And Amelia, man, if you care about her at all, you've got to talk to her."

Tim looked skeptically at Ben. "I don't know. I'm so tired of pretending that everything's perfect, but now it's all fucked up." Frustrated, he pressed his hands to his head, "And as long as we're being honest, I have to admit a lot of this is my fault."

"Which means you can fix it," Ben sipped his coffee giving Tim time to mull it over. "The way I see it you have two choices. You can do nothing and have nothing or anybody meaningful in your life, or grow a pair and show people the real you. I think you'll be pleasantly surprised how much better things are if you give yourself a chance."

"What about my mother?"

"What about her?"

"I walked out on her. Twice." Tim grimaced. Saying it out loud made it seem even worse. "I'm not sure that's something I can fix."

Seconds ticked by as the two sipped their coffees, contemplating Tim's options. "Honestly, I don't see what other choice you have, especially because you're the one who keeps walking away. You have to be the one to reach out first."

Less than thrilled, Tim had to agree. "You're right. I'll do it." A mariachi band boomed loudly in his head, and he wanted to cry. Lesson learned. He would never drink tequila again. "I'll call her…first thing tomorrow."

"Amelia too," Ben reminded, leaving Tim alone to ride out the misery of his hangover. "Let her in or let her go, your choice."

* * *

A quick glance at Tim's watch showed it was 8:05 A.M. Too early to call Pashmina? Or maybe too late. He wished he could turn the clock back that he could have a do over. He would rather be doing anything besides sitting here with clammy hands and a dry throat working up the courage to call his mother. Tim glanced at his watch again, 8:06. He picked up the phone and dialed.

"Hello?" a woman's voice answered on the third ring.

"Pashmina?"

"Yes, who's this?"

"Tim," he answered, offering his surname as an afterthought, "Smith."

A heavy silence followed, and he wondered if taking Ben's advice was a good idea; even the best lawyers can make mistakes. But this wasn't about Ben. "I hope I'm not disturbing you calling so early?" Minus any assurances to the contrary, he forced himself to continue.

"To be perfectly blunt, I've been a total prick." *Idiot!* He slapped his forehead, apologizing for his crudeness, "I'm sorry. Talking to my mother is still pretty new to me."

Pashmina's tender chuckle sounded in his ear. "I know how you feel. I haven't exactly mastered parenting myself---obviously. Maybe we can help each other."

The nervous tension knotting his shoulders eased, and Tim relaxed slightly. "Sounds like a plan to me. Would you like to have lunch some time to talk about it, like maybe today?" He waited eagerly for her to answer.

Pashmina's heart ached and she closed her eyes against the joyful tears welling inside them. Lunch with her son, was there anything better? She pictured a future full of special moments, memories created, celebrations, occasions, his wedding, and grandchildren. There was so much more in store for both of them, but lunch was a very good place to start.

"There's nowhere else I'd rather be," she answered emphatically. "Noon? There's a café across the street from the Dewes building, do you know it?"

"Yep, I've been there plenty of times. I'll see you there at noon." Three hours and forty-five minutes according to the clock on his computer. An eternity. He couldn't wait that long.

"Pashmina, I just want to say that I'm really sorry for the way I treated you. It was a mistake. I was a jerk, but that's not me." Not anymore at least. "I'm starting to realize that you only get what you give in this world, and up till now I've been pretty stingy. I swear I'm going to do my best to change that."

Pashmina shushed him, anxious to set the record straight. "No, I put us in this situation. It was my mistake. I never should have let you go. I thought I was being selfless and giving you a chance at a better life, but it was selfish and stupid. Believe me, if I could go back and make everything right, I would. I'm just so grateful for this second chance."

That was it in a nut shell, no more dwelling on the past or mourning what was lost. It was time to put it all behind her and move on. "Tim, do you still have the St. Barbara medallion I gave you as a baby?"

He fingered the gold disc hanging from his neck. When he was ten, one of the other kids had tried to rip it from him, prompting a beating that left the would-be thief black and blue. It was Tim's medallion, a gift from his mother, and a promise that she would be back for him one day.

"I have it."

Pashmina smiled. "I'm glad. From now on St. Barbara and I will always be with you. I love you, Tim. Always and forever."

The lump in his throat made it hard for Tim to answer. It was like speaking a foreign language, saying the words he had never said to anyone before. "I love you too, Mom."

"See you at noon?"

"Definitely."

CHAPTER EIGHTEEN

It was a picture perfect day for a funeral. Bright sun hung suspended from a cloudless cerulean sky, its warming rays poking gently at the gathering below as a mild breeze whispered soft and cool through the canopy of surrounding trees. Standing on the lawn, lush and green like a spongy carpet, Tim's toes itched to be free from the squeezing confines of his black leather Ferragamo's.

Graveside in the garden that was Forest Hills Cemetery, he surreptitiously scanned the small group surrounding standing there; there was Monte, his iron gaze locked fiercely on the smooth, sleek casket in front of him, as if through sheer will and determination he could bring his beloved friend back to life, and Amelia standing next to him, her arm linked comfortingly through her uncle's but with so many tears streaming down her beautiful face Tim wondered who was supporting whom. Lastly, there was Ben and Chad, two friends and sentries, standing tall and strong, protecting Tim.

In the days following Pashmina's death, Tim had felt lost, drifting aimlessly through a fog of shock and pain. He couldn't believe she was gone. Ben tried to help him through it, showering him with attention and pizza. Tim was ravenous. When was the last time he had eaten? "Eat," Ben ordered, pulling up another chair and grabbing himself a slice. "It's Gino's, your favorite." Not needing any encouragement, Tim sank his teeth into the heavenly ambrosia, almost crying as the delectable flavors of an Italian pie melded in his mouth.

They ate in silence for a time, appeasing their appetites until they were full and Ben asked, "So how're you doing?" A small pucker of worry had nestled snugly between Ben's eyes and Tim was strangely moved. "Sorry, that was a stupid question, how does anyone feel when they lose their mother." Seeing Tim wince, Ben cursed. "Man, I'm sorry, I'm such an idiot."

"Don't apologize. This is all new to me, too. Besides, I can't be mad at the guy who feeds me pizza," Tim joked feebly.

"Thanks." Ben sat quietly for a moment before trying again. "I really am sorry about Pashmina. And Chad and I are going to do everything we can to help you through this."

"Chad?"

"Yeah, he called as soon as he heard." Ben continued, "You know he sort of knows what you're going through, and he's never forgotten what you did for him." Brightening, Ben threw a light punch to Tim's shoulder, "Hey, how many people can say that Chadwick Brown picked up their dry cleaning for them?" He nodded affirmatively at Tim's shocked expression. "Yup, he got your suit, tie, and even had your shoes shined for the funeral. Everything's in your closet ready to go."

A lump formed in Tim's throat, threatening to choke him as tears blurred the sight of Ben's friendly face. "I don't know what to say."

"Hey, Buddy, you don't have to say anything." He patted Tim on the shoulder. "That's what friends are for. Besides, you'd do the same for us."

And Tim knew he would, because despite his best efforts to be a totally self-absorbed prick, he had managed to attract a few visitors to his one man island. He had friends. He just wished it hadn't taken him so long to realize it.

* * *

Masses of people packed the pews of St. John Church, spilling into the aisles and arched alcoves. Outside, loyal fans and curious alike gathered in droves creating their own unofficial service, while local and national news crews reported live from the plaza, their satellite trucks jamming the curbs of Boylston Street and bringing the sounds of morning rush hour to a roaring crescendo. Angry horns and yelling voices created a dull hum that filled the air but Tim was oblivious to it all.

Statue-like he sat numb, equally immune to the presence of the church guests as the blessed saints gazing serenely down upon him from their elaborate stained glass perches encircling the chapel. It was a beautiful church, adorned with ornate gildings of gold and ornamental religious icons, but all Tim could see was Pashmina days earlier, waving as she spotted him waiting for her at the café.

Beautiful as always, she had looked different somehow as she approached the crosswalk, her head high, gaze clear, and it was suddenly obvious. She was happy, totally and completely happy. Gone were the ever-present worry lines penciled between anxious eyes; instead ripple-free pools of rich coffee were sparkling directly at him. Even her posture had changed; she stood taller as though some great weight had been lifted from her.

Watching her, Tim felt different too; nervous but excited like all those Christmas morning's he had spent hoping against hope that Santa would bring him a family of his own. He smiled broadly, white teeth flashing as Pashmina waved to him again. Santa hadn't forgotten him after all.

Pashmina wore a black and white polka dot dress with a black patent leather clutch tucked under one arm and her hair piled high on her head. She was a vision of loveliness. Slipping on a pair of dark glasses, a final touch of chic, she stepped off the curb, eager to reach her lunch date on the other side. Feeling her eyes glued to his face, Tim knew she never saw what hit her.

* * *

"I'm sorry, Mr. Smith, we did everything we could, but your mother's internal injuries were too extensive. We couldn't save her." Dr.

Weinstein looked sympathetically at Tim, sitting bent in a chair, his head firmly in his hands as if to keep it from falling off. The doctor scanned the empty waiting room. "Is there anything we can do for you, someone we can call maybe?"

Tim's shoulders shook silently in response and the doctor sighed. It never got any easier dealing with the loved ones left behind. "There, there, son, everything will be all right," he tried to comfort. "I'll ask one of the nurses to bring your mother's things, just let her know if there's anything else you need, okay? Okay, then," he said. "You take care."

Hours later, when he finally left the hospital, Tim was surprised to find the day had gone, leaving a thick blanket of darkness in its place. He blinked, adjusting his eyes from the harsh hospital fluorescents to the dim of night. What now? Holding tight to the plastic bag with Pashmina's clothes and other personal belongings, he decided to walk back to his apartment.

The evening air felt good on his face and cleared his head enough for him to create a mental check list of all the things he had to do: like call George. Would Pashmina mind? George wasn't exactly one of her favorite people, but she had cared for him once and had his child. He had a right to know. Checking his watch, Tim calculated the nine-hour time difference. It was early in Greece, four o'clock in the morning, but this couldn't wait. He took out his phone and called.

The trilling phone stirred George from sleep, his groggy mind too slow to recognize the sound at first. What the hell? It rang again, sharp and shrill, unaccustomed to announcing callers. No one ever called George, not unless it was an emergency. George's heart stopped. *Tim.* With shaking hands he answered, "Hello?"

"George? It's me, Tim. I'm sorry to wake you."

Relieved, George assured him, "No, no it's okay. What's going on, are you all right?"

"I'm fine. I guess. I just wanted to tell you, to let you know." He took a steadying breath. "Pashmina's dead," he said.

Heavy silence hung between them until his Tim's words finally sank in. "How?" George asked.

"A car accident, this morning." Tim hesitated, unsure what to say. "We were meeting for lunch and she was hit crossing the road."

"You were there?" George wanted to yell, to hit something. How had this happened? Pashmina was gone. He would never see her again. And Tim, he had lost his mother, the woman he had been searching for all his life, the woman he had just found. George gripped the phone tightly, thankful for the connection, however small. "I'll be there as soon as I can," he promised. "I'll contact the airlines right away and let you know when I get to Boston. Don't worry, I'll take care of everything."

Tim's eyes closed in relief. "Thank you. You've no idea how much that means to me." After twenty-nine years it felt good to let someone else take charge. "But I need to do this. I want to do this, for my mother. It's all I can do for her now."

George nodded, understanding. "I'll reach out to her family here. They never knew about us--either of us--but it's time they did. They'll want to meet their grandson and nephew."

And Tim wanted to meet them. He had planned to talk to Pashmina about that, about going to Greece together. And then she died. "Thank you," he choked.

Tim's sobs tore at his heart as George forced himself to be strong. "Remember, Tim, you're not alone. I'm here for you."

* * *

Compared to the chaos of the church, the burial service was a haven of peace and quiet. "Holy God, Holy Mighty, Holy and Immortal, have mercy on us," the Trisagion prayer pierced Tim's thoughts, reminding him where he was and why. "Holy God, Holy Mighty, Holy and Immortal, have mercy on us," the priest chanted a third time, commencing the traditional burial prayer. A light breeze lifted the dark curls from Tim's neck leaving goose bumps on his skin. Shivering slightly, he dug his chilled hands deep into his pockets, his fingers curling protectively around the crisp folded edges of origami hiding inside. Pashmina's letter.

Mixed in with all the condolence cards, bills, and junk that served as his mail, Pashmina's loving declaration inscribed on her personal stationary was all he had left of his mother. He had nearly missed it, mindlessly sorting through the stack, flipping important stuff onto the table, the rest in the trash, until he came across one addressed to him in bold and elegant cursive. He knew who it was even before the soft scents of white orchid and vanilla wafted over him.

But he didn't read it right away; partly because not knowing made him feel like she was still alive and partly because her voice from the dead kind of creeped him out. She must have mailed it the morning she died. But eventually, curiosity got the better of him, and he retreated to the privacy of his room to hear what she had to say.

My Darling *Son*, Pashmina began, three words that made it hard to read the rest through brimming tears, but Tim pushed himself to finish it. It was a gift, he realized, something that gave him more pleasure and less pain each time he read it. And he read it over and over until he worried it might disintegrate. Then he tucked it into his pocket for safekeeping. He didn't have to read it anymore. He had memorized every word.

CHAPTER NINETEEN

"Hi." Wearing a suit and holding a bouquet of flowers, Tim felt more like an awkward prom date than a penitent suitor. Over the past few days he had managed to make amends with almost everyone he really cared about except Amelia, intentionally saving her for last. It was a risk, but she was the most important one and truthfully, the one that scared him the most. Losing her was unimaginable.

Judging from her stony expression, however, she didn't have a problem with cutting him loose. "Hi."

"How are you?" he asked, really wanting to know. The apartment door began to close and he put a hand out to stop it. "Please, Amelia. Baby, please just hear me out and I promise I'll never bother you again."

Like him, Amelia still wore her funeral clothes from earlier, minus her conspicuously missing high heeled shoes. He smiled slightly. She hated 'dress up' shoes. Weapons disguised as fashion statements she called them once, rubbing her aching feet after a long day in black patent stilettos. If a woman really wanted to torture a man, all she would have to do is make him walk in a pair of her shoes for an hour.

But Amelia was the one looking tormented now. Her usual peaches and cream complexion was ashen, dark circles formed half-moons beneath red-rimmed eyes; she looked sad and weary and wounded. Guilt pricked at his skin making it burn, and he ran a nervous hand through his hair. This was his fault.

As if she heard him, the door opened, and Amelia grudgingly waved him inside. Wasn't this what she wanted? An explanation, an apology, both. They were long overdue and he was here, finally. There was no way in hell she was letting him go now, not until he manned up and told her everything.

Stepping back, Amelia made sure he could pass without touching her, keeping her expression carefully blank to mask the emotional coup threatening inside her. Despite all of the crap he had pulled and how much she hated him right now, the guy could still turn her inside out with just a glance from those gorgeous chocolate eyes of his; his mother's eyes.

Pashmina. Amelia felt the same familiar ache in her chest as when her dad died. Gone too soon. It wasn't fair. "Life's not always fair, Amelia," her mother had said, "some days are better, some are worse, but they're never the same." Tucking a strand of hair behind her daughter's ear, Francesca had smiled bravely, "It's you and me now, Sweetheart, but Daddy will always be with us and we'll always be lucky we had him in our lives, even if it was only for a little while." Pashmina, too. She was a wonderful woman and a wonderful friend for the short time they had known each other. For the second time in her life Amelia counted her blessings.

Feeling invisible, Tim touched her arm, squeezing lightly to get her attention. "I know I have a lot of explaining to do." He hesitated, "I'm just not sure where to start."

Unmoved, Amelia plopped herself on the couch. "Well, don't look at me. I've got my own problems to worry about." She'd be damned if she was going to make this easy for him.

"I know you do," he agreed quickly, "I just hope I'm one of those problems." Amelia's eyebrows spiked in surprise, and he realized his mistake. That didn't come out right. "What I mean is, I hope you still care enough about me for me to be a problem to you." He placed an emphatic hand over his heart, "I know I've been an idiot, a jerk, an asshole." Amelia motioned for him to keep going, and he laughed nervously.

"Seriously, there's no excuse for the way I've treated you. I screwed it all up and then some, but I swear if you'll just give me a chance, I'll explain everything." He scanned her face for signs of a winter thaw, a softening in her eyes, tight lips relaxing into full bloom, something, anything encouraging.

Like a statue, Amelia gazed at him, passively attentive, and Tim began to sweat. He moved to the couch, not trusting his legs to hold him much longer and took her hands in his. "Baby, I love you. I think I've loved you since our first date when you let me off the hook." He shook his head in disbelief, "I was a jerk even then but you stayed with me anyway."

Amelia nodded breaking her silence, "Rose would say it wasn't one of my finer moments."

One more fence he had to mend if he had the chance. "Rose is a good friend. She really looks out for you."

"I've got Rose and you've got Ben."

"I know," he agreed. "No matter how shitty I was to him, Ben's always been there for me. I didn't deserve a friend like him or a girlfriend like you either but that was before. Meeting my parents helped me find the real me, not some make believe version I convinced myself I was. The old me was too scared to get close to anybody, but I've never wanted anything more than I want you now. Please, Amelia, don't let me go."

Despite her resolve to stay strong, Amelia could feel herself slipping. She had never seen him like this before: open, honest, vulnerable. More than anything she wanted to go to him but it wasn't that easy. "You lied to me," she said. "And you used me. And you didn't trust me. Everyone knew it, Pashmina, Monte, Ben, Rose, even my manicurist tried to tell me. But I didn't believe them. I believed you. And now you're asking me to believe you again."

When had her life become such a sappy soap opera? Disgusted, she stood tall, meeting his chest, and demanded, "Why should I trust you after everything you've done?"

Excellent question. "I'm sorry, I can't answer that." He pleaded with her to understand, "I can't say why you should take a chance on me, I only know that my heart is breaking right now 'cause I'm so scared you won't." Taking her by the shoulders, he promised, "I swear to God if you stay with me, I will never do anything ever again to make you regret your decision."

Somewhere nearby a clock ticked loudly, tick tock, tick tock, marking time as Tim waited anxiously for her answer. Hearing it too, Amelia had had enough. No more wasted time. Wrapping her arms around him, she pulled him close, breathing the familiar scent of aftershave and Tim, like clean air in the wake of a storm.

She hugged him tightly. "Never is an awfully long time," she whispered.

"I'm counting on it," he replied.

EPILOGUE

My Darling Son,

If you know nothing else about me you need to know this: I love you. I always have and I always will.

My mother, your grandmother, said these words to me when I left home for America so many years ago. Her only daughter was leaving, and it broke her heart. A mother's not supposed to have a favorite child, but I knew I was hers. It was her secret. I wished so much that I could tell her mine, that I could tell her I was pregnant, that I was scared, but I was ashamed; not of you, of me. I had become a person neither of us could be proud of.

I think she knew, though, mothers have an odd way of knowing these things. She did the best she could to help, sending St. Barbara along to protect me. St. Barbara was the only reason I was able to release you to what I hoped would be a better life. I placed the chain with her medallion around your sweet neck and promised that she'd protect you always. And she did keep you physically safe. I was the one who failed you. Miserably.

My father once said there's a sinner and a saint in all of us, but I never really understood what he meant until now. You see, sometimes we do bad things in the name of doing good. I've made bad choices, I've been selfish, and I've hurt many people. Unfortunately, many of my wrongs can't be made right. And I have to live with that.

But there are others I can correct, beginning with my worst offense: giving you up. I promise that I will spend the rest of my life making it up to you, being a mother who adores you, supports you, and I will tackle anyone who tries to harm you. I know I'm coming very late to the party, but I hope with all my heart that you'll welcome me into your life as your mother, your friend, and your biggest fan.

Darling, it's a very rich man who's blessed with good friends and a woman who loves him like Amelia loves you. If I can give you a bit of motherly advice, hold onto them tightly. They are your family, they have your back, and you must have theirs. They are a precious commodity to be treasured. Don't be afraid to let them know it.

Loving you now and forever,
Mom

###

Acknowledgements

Second Chances was a true leap of faith; not just for us, but for our families and friends who supported, encouraged, inspired, and spurred us on through the four long years it took to complete this journey. 'Thanks' isn't nearly enough to express how much we appreciate you and what you've given us. From Santas Martha and Debbie who gave us some of our first writing tools, to Patti who dared to read and critique what no one had before, to Carson our technology guru whose talents brought us to life online, the list is too long to name them all but we hope you know who you are and that we couldn't have done this without you.

We'd be remiss if we didn't give a special shout out to our loving husbands and sons. On days when the road we walk seems an endless vertical climb, we simply remember all of your love, support, and sacrifice, and our sanity is once again restored. You're the best. We love you.

About the Authors

Often mistaken for sisters, Leigh and Victoria consider themselves twins from different mothers. They met on the sidelines of their sons' baseball games, and quickly bonded over books, baseball politics, and Mrs. Brown's 'famous chocolate chip cookies.' Not surprisingly, their decision to write a book together also came about over a pizza dinner, and they've been sharing a love for writing and eating ever since.

This is their first literary collaboration. Learn more about them by visiting their website http://browncorlissbooks.com, and look for their second novel, *The Pie Sisters*, coming in 2014.

Leigh and Victoria both live with their families in Rhode Island.

Made in the USA
Charleston, SC
28 July 2014